stories

short prose

though
most of it is not fiction
it is reportage

by

Norman Allan

Stories©
by Norman Allan
self-published on/in/at/by amazon's createspace POD
1st first draft "published" 12th June 2015
1st edit 22rd June 2015
2nd edit 5th July 2015
3rd edit 9th July 2015

ISBN-13:
978-1514345054

ISBN-10:
1514345056

This is for

Flynn
Matty
Leo
Soren
Tarn

specially in case
any of you become a publisher
or an academic specializing in
short stories and prose sketches,

or more simply,
incase any of you find an interested
in what that strange grandpa wrote…

I hope you enjoy these
whenever

CONTENTS

INTRODUCTION

I might say his/my shorter prose might only be significant in the context of his/my other work, some of the longer fiction, the art, the natural philosophy (ultradilution/homeopathy work in particular), and if you came to esteem my poetry, for instance, then you might, I pray, find my short pieces interesting, and sometimes delightful. Just yesterday I was telling Linda that *Betsy's Goddess* (page 29) is a perfect prose piece. It's 171 words! That far, once, we made it!

These are short stories and prose sketches, and stuff, written over the decades. *Symptoms* is a highly fictionalized autobiographical piece. *Time Travel* is fiction, science fiction. Is *Dialoging and Imaging in a Clinical Setting* a story or an essay, an article? It's almost a story. I'm putting it in this draft. Then we'll see... All the rest is, what I'd call, "reportage": things I've observed, stories I thought worth telling, and they are told in the first person : that's how I write.

A propos of the first person singular... *Wikisays*...

turn the page

SO'HAM

wiki-says:

so'ham **is an emphatic form of** *aham*, the first-person pronoun ("I")

aham = I	*asmi* = am
AHAM ASMI	I AM

and: wikisays...

"Some say that when a child is born it cries *Koham-Koham* which means Who am I? That is when the universe replies *So'ham*."

GRANDMOTHER CROW

In 1970 Bill Crow was a graduate student. He shared an office next to mine. Bill Crow was one quarter native: his grandmother was full blooded Cheyenne. After the Indian Wars, the army had herded the Cheyenne into two camps. Bill's grandmother was eleven years old in the 1880s when the army marched the eleven hundred remnants in the southern camp a thousand miles, in the middle of winter, to the northern camp. Only one hundred of those eleven hundred souls survived the march, and these included Bill's grandmother.

Bill was a student during the Vietnam war - he was studying in psychology at Berkeley - and he was a member of the radical SDS (Students for a Democratic Society). When he graduated he got his draft notice. He decided to come north to Canada to do postgraduate work and to avoid participating in what he saw as an unjust war.

Before coming north Bill went home to Mobile to see his family. Granny was in her eighties and he wasn't sure if he would see her again. He went in to Granny to tell her he was going to Canada to dodge the draft. Granny said: "You'll come back for the war, though, won't you?"

CATCHING BUTTERFLIES

Crazy Jane had nothing to hide: it all depended on what was on the agenda. When she smiled at me my heart fountained.

I met her up on the Downs on a sunny May Day. Her face lit and I fell into her smile. I'm prone to that. The story I want to tell is of Crazy Jane Farr and of what she said to me, her last parting words in Churchill Square; but to get there I'll have to speak of our meeting, and of the "Free".

Take two

I just made a connection of Jane to another Brighton clique beyond the Free. To the Unicorn Book shop and Geophrey Harrison. In the back of my "I Ching" I find her address care of Geoff. Jane connects through Geophrey to Ann Clark whose daughter Michelle's hamster Jane butchered! Now that was crazy. But does it necessarily mean that the later attack on the psychotherapist was driven by anger? I think not.

I met Jane in May on Cissbury Tor, over the hill back towards the sea from Cissbury Ring above Worthing. Nick the Druid had organised a small spring free bop. (How was it bankrolled? Did record companies in those days of yore sponsor little festivals?) I met Crazy Jane on Cissbury Tor, and her face lit up. A frank face. A trim body. Crazy Jane, bright as a pin. Though battered, she opened to me like the heavens, and I fell into her smile.

"Where do I know you from?" I asked.

"St. Francis," we both replied. St. Francis is the big head hospital beyond "H block". I had visited St. Francis through my involvement with PNP, and the Free. I had spent much of the prior two years on the fringe of the Free, and through this I was visiting the hospital where Jane was incarcerated after the Copenhagen incident. I was the incumbent chairperson, incorporation of PNP, People Not Psychiatry, a support group sponsored by the Free. You see, when I had returned to Brighton I had been drawn to the Free like a moth, and Dale had said, "If you really want to help, then take on PNP. I haven't got the time, Otto hasn't got the bedside manner, and Jon just wants to be a Manhattan Queen."

In practice PNP was a once a week tea and sympathy evening at the Free Times cafe, and a once a week visit to St. Francis. Jon and Ros, who with Dale and Otto, were the heart of the Free, visited St. Francis with me once to see Jane, and thus we'd met. A brief and neutral encounter.

Why was I visiting the nut house week after week? Well, Dale had set me up for it, and I couldn't refuse. Since childhood I had told myself that I wanted to understand the "mind". I had for a long time felt that an insane asylum would be an important place to try to sniff out "mind" for mind would surely reveal itself where it was batting its little brain against some crazies skull. But I had procrastinated. I had never poked my nose behind those walls. So for six months I became PNP, and visited the bug house, and found that it smells of stale urine, and feels like a railway station with no trains running. Just time crawling on and on, like bugs on a wall.

Then a winter and a marriage gone I went up to Cissbury fair, and there in May met sweet Jane. "Where do I know you from?" I asked. "St. Francis," we replied. We beamed at each other. Don't ask me why. And I felt that I had met my sister. I guess I was just so pleased to see her joy in meeting me. She asked what I was doing, and I told her of my plans to travel. "I'm looking for where to go. I may just have found the keys to Marrakech."

One of my projects was writing a fairytale. "Pipedreams" was set in part in Marrakech, and I had never been. Just before, up there on the tor, I had bumped in to Mike the chauffeur who had said he had an apartment in Marrakech. I should have known better. He gave me the address and the name of the girl who was looking after it for him. A fictitious address, it would transpire, and he got the girl's name wrong too. It was MacDonaugh, not MacDuff, and she had never heard of Mike when nonetheless I found her. But back on the tor I thought I'd travel to Morocco and invited Jane to join me.

"Can't. Home Office impounded my passport. It's cost me two hundred quid to get it back, to cover the air-fare from Copenhagen and two attendants. It's a long story."

"I've time."

"No, another time. Tell me more of you."

I told Jane of my plans, and I told her of my actions, of writings done and writings planned. "I'm researching the Free for a novel. I've got lots of bits and pieces, and I've got a title: "The Fringe of the Free"."

The Free bears explaining. The Free Times was a cafe in Brighton, and was also a species of alternative Welfare Service. The Free were Dale and Jon and Otto. Otto's mummy had the money.

When I met Dale in Brighton some years prior he was *en famille* with a couple of his ex-lovers, Jon and Otto,. Together they would constitute the core of the Free family. At that time, 1970, they opened a Free Times cafe with a theatre space, and theatre. Kay, my wife, and Jon hit it off - there was clearly some possibly sexual glue - and while we where away in Canada, a year, they corresponded. After that year, and a further year of chasing my tail in the Irish countryside - what other solution was there to the world's problems than to develop extended family and communal endeavour. I thrashed around ineptly at engagement, lost a year, a portion of my wife's small inheritance, and the last shreds of her regard.

The Free drew us back to Brighton; Kay to Jon quite simply, and I, in part to Jon's glamour and enthusiasm, and more, to Dale's posture of involvement and adventure. So we returned to Brighton, and to the fringe of the Free. And I became PNP.

By this time the Free was a Brighton institution. The theatre space had closed, and Dale and family had moved the cafe inland, back from the sea. They leased a corner property and opened a new Free Times cafe. So they ran a cafe and a mini-welfare service. There was a "crash service": they kept a list of people who would be prepared to offer short term hospitality to those in emergency need of accommodation. This was the occasional battered wife, or chucked-out husband, as I was soon to be, but for the greater part it was itinerant youths drifting away from home and with gravity trickling down from London to Brighton.

Dale also offered legal counseling: primarily tenant counseling and drug bust, though I recall him arranging bail, for instance, for a young girl jailed for lifting a milk bottle from someone's doorstep. Where necessary Dale would arrange lawyers, though usually he managed the counseling himself.

Jon, Dale's "Manhattan Queen", though gay thrived on female company. All the time I knew him there was a female companion. With Kay's removal from the scene (our journeys to Canada and Ireland), Jon hooked up with Roslyn. Ros was a princess. Not that she was royal in the literal sense, nor was she stuck up, or needy greedy. Rather she was charisma incarnate. A human magnet.

Through her luster the Free shone. Jon and Ros and a changing group of friends ran a vegetarian cafeteria on the University campus: the major source of income of the Free, beyond the welfare that most of them claimed.

In this space on campus they held parties, though maybe "dances" is a better description for one paid to gain entrance, and one danced. Danced to the Grateful Dead. The Dead were God to Jon, Ros and their side of the Free. Dale, for his part, might turn up at the bops, put in his appearance shy and lost and at the same time looking like Napoleon. Though fair and balding, he was short, and bore a brooding dignity. Probably the most Bonaparte about him was a tendency to slide one arm inside his jacket. But once one had seen this likeness, it stuck. Dale would come to the parties and look out of place. He was much more at home in the cafe reading the real estate (always looking for a better place), or in his aerie above the Free Times, sitting amidst his orange-crate furniture analysing the city and the world, reducing or expanding them with an acerbic humour.

Here he collected the flotsam and jetsam of Great Britain. Adolescence fled or driven from home, or just bursting free to tumble down to Brighton lost. Dale himself had been picked up and restored from near death in his adolescence, and so now perhaps in recompense he hung out with the needy, and patched more than a few through their destitution. I suppose, too, the access to pretty boys was a perk of the trade, though Stephane said he held him chastely, so the inference may be unkind.

Meanwhile Jon and Ros and pals pulsed party glamour. They formed an inner court of the Free. A court of grace, a court of plenty. So a schism grew between the party crew and the welfare Free, Dale and Otto. Then in '74 Dale and Ros surprised us all when out of the blue they announced their engagement. A stately marriage ceremony in St. Michael's cathedral-like church was a fitting climax to the soap opera. Ros and Dale ran off to Wales to raise chickens and children. "They ran off with the fucking car," grumbled Otto. Brighton was free of the Free, and I began to collect data on this phenomenon that had so seduced me. That would be the spring of 1974, when I went up to Cissbury Tor, and met Jane.

"The Free," said Jane. "Now I could tell you some stories."

Jane started off as Ros's friend, and this pulled her into the group loving, and 'tripping', and then as things evolved Jane ended up sort of servicing Otto at Free's laid back orgies (Laid back? Laid back and front.)

Acid and the Grateful Dead were a sacred rite with the party Free, Jon, Ros and friends. Jane had at this time been institutionalised once, after the mania and mayhem of the massacre of Michelle's hamster, and because of this one might say she was in some sense in the care of the Free when they took her up to London on the Holy trip, turned her on with 250 micrograms of primo acid - orange sunset, tangerine dream, some cute name - and they lost her, abandoned her at the Grateful Dead concert, Wembley Arena, twelve thousand people, 1972. It lefty Jane crazy, again.

Oh how the mighty fall. What virtue was left to these knights of the Counter Culture? How fucking disappointing! However, what my meeting with Jane left me with was not so much disillusionment with my cardboard Camelot heroes, but a glow from my encounter with Jane. I know that between two people there are always barriers and limits, but oft time in our first meetings we don't yet meet them, and it feels as though there is no boundary, we are in one harmony, bliss! better than a kiss. We exchanged phone numbers, and said we would meet again.

It was four days later that I heard from Jane. She phoned after midnight to say that she had broken a mirror and slashed her wrists with the shards. She couldn't face the hospital. They'd lock her up. Could I come?

That was the one lie Jane told me, for when the taxi took me back into Brighton, twelve nighttime country miles from Burgess Hill, though the mirror was shattered with splintered glass scattered, Jane's wrists were intact. She just didn't trust herself to pick up the pieces, or to survive in the gloom of her glass filled room. The gloom of days and night and life. Or was it a simple "block", a clean up the mess block? Throwing the ashtray at the mirror is no great triumph of the will, but it's something. Picking up the mess is so dreary, why go on: pick up the glass and slash.

I picked up the pieces, made her tea, and talked. Then we lay clothed and entwined, and perhaps we dozed before the dawn soon rose. It was hard for me to see Jane as insane for her aura was always clear while I was there. Impulsive, this was the weakness that in bad times took her beyond the brink to the shrink. What I found was a troubled friend; a refugee. In me there is a need to serve, and to love (when I find someone dear). I found Jane open, vulnerable and lovely. No barriers, still. She made herself translucent, if not transparent.

In the morning we breakfasted in a greasy spoon and felt as real as all those truckers. We hitched a ride to Burgess Hill, sat in my room and just smiled. Held hands walking down to the kitchen, cooked lunch and felt at home. Then we spent the afternoon in the May meadows. Bluebells like blue stars in the green sky meadow bank with the dark woods rising behind turning us into archetypes, boy and girl, meadow and spring. We touched hands, but not lips: there was no urgency.

In the evening again we lay together. This time we shed our clothes like old skin. And she let me in. But it started as no pleasure to her, so we stopped.

Jane had been on the game, and even without that sex is such a coin in our civilization that it often confounds relationship. Was it then that she told me about the Copenhagen airport?

During her second hospitalization, that which followed the Dead Concert, Jane was in therapy with a pleasant and intelligent young man who helped her some, and with whom she communicated easily. After her release, hastened perhaps by his thoughtful therapy, the sessions continued on an outpatient basis. One day the therapist invited Jane to come touring with him through Denmark in his Volkswagen camper. "No," said Jane. She couldn't go with him because she didn't feel "that way" about him.

"You misunderstand. It's not like that," he protested. He wanted her company. And he persuaded her that indeed it was simply friendship that he sought: they got on so well together. So off they went touring Denmark.

But it wasn't like that. He was constantly courting her and pestering. On the third day - would they be or not be at Ellsinore - wherever they were, Jane had had it! She told him to turn the bus around and take her back to the airport. She told him that if he tried to cop another feel she would kill him.

They got to the airport. She got her ticket. They were in the lobby saying goodbye, and he tried to grope her one last time. All she had to do was push him away, to scream, to walk away and get on the plane, and, and he would have learned nothing. He might try the same scam on the next comely patient: might hurt some innocent. All Jane needed to do to escape herself was to get on the plane. But she took a knife out of her handbag, and stabbed him!

He spent a few days in hospital, and maybe learned a lesson. Jane went home in handcuffs escorted by two white coated attendants, and spent a year in the St. Frances Hospital, Haywards Heath, where I met her.

I've told this story, the Copenhagen airport, many times, because I think it's important. Almost as important as walking camels. Some of those I tell the story to say Jane stabbed him out of anger, rage, but I don't think so. I don't think she stabbed him to hurt him, or to hurt herself, to put herself back in hospital. I think she stabbed him out of compassion. It was a sacrifice to save him and save others, to teach him not to fuck about with a sacred trust when entrusted with fragile souls. I really think it was a noble act, selfless love, and honouring of self (though I'm probably the only one who ever saw it that way... Jane didn't. Jane didn't have an opinion. She just did it).

So we didn't make love. We slept curled up together, like babes in the wood. With the morning we walked again amid the meadows, banks of flowers, bluebells, lush green above and behind the smoky black of tree trunks rising above the bank, the trees still leafless, though burgeoning with bud. Hand in hand but going where? I gave it no thought, just pleased to share.

Jane went back into town in the afternoon - some affairs to look after - and we arranged to meet at her place the next morning. So eleven o'clock next morning I arrived and walked in - the door was open - and found her fucking. In flagro with some swarthy fellow, squat and hairy and humping her. Some acquaintance from her gutter life in London. He made his living owning and running slot-machines .

"Excuse me!" I walked out into the kitchen to wait. Jane threw on a housecoat and came to explain. No apology, just "it's better this way." Thanks a lot. I believe the message was meant to be that she didn't feel she deserved me, could hold me, could have me, could serve me. I felt disappointment, sad, but I felt no betrayal. I did feel relief. And I wondered at her caring. Honesty deserves honesty. Caring deserves caring. Jane was straight with me. And just as I think Jane was selfless with the therapist, I know she was honest and caring with me. She tried to save our friendship and our honesty from what she felt was impossible; that we could be together for any length of time.

Jane told her "friend" she had some chores, and dressed, and we went out and walked. A silent walk of missed love, of "how close, but..." We walked all the way to Brighton's then new and sterile downtown Mall, Churchill Square. We stood by metal railings, painted grey, marking the edge not of the world I know but simply of the shopping centre, centre of Brighton, edge of our small meeting. The sky contracted: grew grey into my heart. Limits. We wake from another dream, empty. She readied to leave. And I had no argument except "I love you", or "I want you", and they were lame. They didn't walk, they wouldn't work, so I stayed silent.

"If you want to catch a butterfly," she said, "you have to be a professional." And with that she walked away.

Concerning "Catching Butterflies"

This was my first short story. I wrote it in the late eighties for Lea Harper – I guess to say that I knew something about fumbling after butterflies.

The Leonard Cohen story/poem below speaks of Lea, and of my father. My father, Ted, had a great influence on my writing. He encouraged me to write. Started me… That was in the mid-seventies. I've written a little about that in the introduction/ preface to "Symptoms", later in this collection.

He also suggested the title for preceding story. The first drafts were titled "Crazy Jane". "That won't work," Ted said. "Too many people have used it. Yeats… How about 'Catching Butterflies'".

THE BOURGEOIS BLUES
My Leonard Cohen Story

This concerns Lee Harper's amazing first poetic outpouring,
which my father sent to Leonard Cohen. Lee was, and is,
beautiful, so Ted enclosed a "head shot".
  A few days later Ted said to me, "You write poetry," and the
something like, "Wow! Your good. You're really good", and he
sent my poetry to Leonard.
  Leonard said he didn't think that I had transcended my
bourgeois upbringing. He also pointed out that Ted hadn't send
my "head shot".
  So I wrote Leonard "a bourgeois blues".

The bourgeois blues have spread
way beyond Vienna.
Yesterday they rolled
under my bedroom door.
They crept up my William Morris wallpaper,
down the velvet drapes;
they stained the sheets
and ate my gladiola.

Leonard thinks I'm bathed in it.
Leonard thinks he's free,
But I know we're swimming
through the Company's dross.
This ain't the Jordan
in which we've been tossed.
It's the vomit of ages.

Babylon is a large mother.

Yesterday the bourgeois blues
rolled under my door.
Today I'll wash the curtain,
and hope there ain't no more.

*Ted read the poem to Leonard over the phone and Leonard
said, "Read it again."*

HEROES

I would have sworn it was here, but it's gone. My yesterdays. I'm trying to remember one of my heroes, Spanish Frank, but what do I keep of him? What does the world keep? Twelve children he says. I can't even conjure up his face.

I do remember Spanish Frank's motorbike. Frank found the bike buried beneath cinders walking round to the side of a friend's back garden. He dug it free. It was a Triumph Thunderbird, a fifty three, rusted almost beyond recognition but, to Frank, a promise of freedom. Frank took her home in bits. In the following days and nights he cleaned and polished each piece. He bore the shafts by hand, fitted high-lift cams, and a distance piece with a viewer for the carburettor - this last is a petrol reserve for long corners. He decorated the tank with a lightning motif, and painted the frame a fiery red. He stood back to admire his artefact - this glistening dream - this thing of power.

"I christen you Nemesis," he said.

The first time Frank mounted Nemesis and kicked her over she spluttered, but neither caught nor died. The petrol feed? Frank leaned over to look in the "viewer" of the distance piece he'd thoughtfully installed. The petrol's flowing, he saw, and in that instant the engine caught and surged, spiralling Frank through the air to the ground. Nemesis suffered little, leaping the curb and through the shop window of the corner tobacconist. Frank says he had to laugh, despite the pain, and the damages. Frank sported a crutch, one foot bandaged, the first time I saw him outside the Free Times Cafe. He was leaning lightly on the crutch, with his white hair a lion's mane, then in his mid forties, a handsome man, not big, or grand - but with a substantial feeling.

My getting to know Frank came through the Free's crash

service and life's catastrophe. In the early nineteen seventies the Free ran an alternative welfare system. A major item was the crash service. They had a list of those who'd offer accommodation for a night or, like the Arabs, up to three nights. Then one had to move on, till one found some resolve, or exhausted the system.

A while after my return to Brighton - drawn to Brighton by the Free like moths - my first marriage floundered - another story. She threw me out. I went up to the Free, to their crash service and spent my first nights away from home with Spanish Frank.

Frank lived in a basement in St. Michael's Terrace. I slept on his sofa. We sat up late into the night and talked. During the evening, he played Flamenco guitar, of course, and he played a recording of Bach, a canto where the organ builds tone on tone, till overtones roared with one another. "Better than rock and roll," he said. I conceded. And then he told me the following story, how he got his name.

The East End of London, after the depression, before the war, had no savour for young Frank Lewis. The war though, promised excitement and escape. At fifteen, Franklin lied about his age and enlisted in the Merchant Navy, which was the fastest freight out of London. In the wartime, all sailors were Royal Navy and under fire. That didn't faze young Frank. "It's a man's world," he said, chest swelling. And away from Europe, to begin with, there were long weeks of implacable ocean.

Frank sailed off to the Orient. In Shanghai, he went ashore with friends, to an opium den. "If that little chinaman can smoke that stuff, so can I," thought Frank. And telling the story, his face relaxed, quietened. "I had a thousand dreams," he said, "and all of them were bad."

It was in Shanghai that he bought the little green jade Buddha that was to become his love charm, and his luck charm. I will speak of it later.

On a hot night in the summer of '43, Frank's ship was torpedoed in the English channel. As far as he knows, Frank was the only survivor. He was washed up on the Brittany shore. In the morning, he found three German soldiers swimming, found their clothes and weaponry amongst some rocks and cover. Killed them. He didn't go into details, but one by one he took out the rest of the German soldiers on the bay - twelve in all. These killings outraged him. He felt empty like the corpses and he vowed he'd replace them - that he would sire twelve children.

Demobbed after the war, civvies street looked dull. The only interesting niche seemed to be larceny, so Frank became a thief, graduating from corner shops to banks. For fifteen years he lived the life of a villain. The main drawback, he said, was that villains were boring people. The other problem was getting nicked. No problem for fifteen years. During this time Frank generated twelve children by twelve women, before getting nabbed for armed robbery. He was sent down for eight years. He served six, this in Parkhurst maximum security. He spent four years in solitary. He preferred his own company. Found it dependable.

About six months before he was due parole, someone brought him in a tab of LSD. A turning point. To be trite, Frank saw life as though it were new, alive, breathing, and he loved it so much he let the chips fall off his shoulders. He decided thence forth to live an affirmation of delight. Next day he wrote a letter to a friend begging them to bring him a guitar, and in the remaining six months in jail he taught himself to play. He no longer resented being in prison. It gave him the time he needed make changes, and learn new ways. After his release, he went down to Spain to study Flamenco. There after his friends called him 'Spanish Frank'.

Spanish Frank returned to England in '69, and made his living as a roofer. When I met him in 1972, his guitar playing, the Flamenco, was quite wonderful. He was damn near a virtuoso. And though he didn't sing, in his grunts and *oles*, you could smell the gypsy campfires, and the sour wine of the taverns. I once ask him why he didn't play professionally. "Sometimes," he said, "when you try to turn a pleasure into a business, you end up with a heartache. I know that this is a solace for me, and if sometimes its a pleasure for my friends, well..." He shrugged.

Frank was still mending roofs years later, when I met up with him again in Wales. We drove over to a valley where Frank was mending some stonewalled outbuildings which, in Wales, they call barns. A high wind had lifted and shifted its black slate roof. The day, that morning, was warm and sunny - the one piece of sun I saw in my whole three weeks in Wales that spring. Frank took off his coat, and threw a line over the roof. He was just going to pull it back up onto the wall with the tractor. I was surprised that it was such a simple procedure. "That's how it's done," he said.

We walked round to the back of the buildings to secure the line round the main beam and to inspect and release the supports which Frank had put the day before to shore up the roof and stop it shifting further. As I helped him by untying one of the support, he drew my attention to urgent consequences. "Take the line in front of you, not behind. You needn't risk tangling in it, even for a moment. If the support, there, gave way ..." he left the rest unsaid.

In the afternoon we were driving back to the cottage Frank was renting, driving in his old ford van through the loins of the Carmarthen hills, narrow roads tunnelling through shrouded trees into the twilight. Though forenoon had been sunny, now drizzle and vapours wrapped grey around us. "We're back in Wales," I said. On the dashboard there was that small jade Buddha. I asked Frank about it. Could I handle it. Pick it up? "Sure." He explained how he had bought it during the war, as a lad, in Shanghai. I asked him if it had religious connotations for him, or if it was a good luck charm. "More of a love charm," he said, and he explained that he used is to stimulate his amours in foreplay to the threshold of climax.

We stopped at a crossroads corner shop. I bought bread, butter and Marmite. I'd just discovered Marmite. As we drove on, I dabbed my fingers into the brown paste. Frank leaned across and scooped his little finger in. "Hmm," he grunted.

"This salt kills babies."

We turned off the little highway onto a country lane, tortuous in trees and fog. "Last week," said Frank, "I drove off the road here. I just turned the wheel and drove into the ditch. A moment later, a sports car shot round this corner. I would have been annihilated. A total catastrophe."

"Maybe you heard it coming. Heard it humming, subliminally Some vibration"

"Perhaps. It happened another time. Not the same bit of road, but the same thing. I just drove into the ditch and swish. I don't think I heard, but whatever. I follow my hunches."

It wasn't the drama of Frank's life that drew me to him. It was a calmness, a warmth and a solidity he carried, that served me as a model in my transition from a dazed youth to the next struggles: a calm that still eludes me. And Frank was a hero to me, but again not because of the spice and storm in his history. My heroes are people who overcome adversity to make something meaningful of their life. Not something grand. But they take back control, usually in a simple way. Just being. Frank was the first of these models. Crazy Jane was probably the second, though I didn't know it at the time. Not until seventeen years later, when we met again. I'm going to speak of Crazy Jane, for her story twines with Spanish Frank.

I went back to Brighton last summer after twelve years away. A maze of memories - these hills, that house - I've lived all over this town. Hanging out with my kids, this time round, I stepped back not twelve, but twenty-five years, back into my habits of the sixties, sitting round walls, smoking, walking the beach collecting pebbles, walking the town - I bumped into shining Neil. "How do you find Brighton after so long?" he asked. I said it looked seedy. "It's always looked seedy," he said. Twelve years back, when Neil was experiencing God in a guru, he was walking round in a loin cloth with wild open eyes. I tried again to penetrate his eyes. We managed a smile, but the eyes were surface, flat; their lustre gone.

I quizzed Neil about old friends. Did he know of this one or that? Did he know of Spanish Frank? "Frank Lewis? He died sometime in the early eighties. Crashed his bike."

I sat a moment.

"And Crazy Jane?" I asked.

"The one with the kid? She moved to Lewis."

"No, the blond girl." There had been at least two Crazy Janes in our circle of acquaintances in those days. (Everyone knows a Crazy Jane, though not everyone knows Yeats.)

"Oh, that Crazy Jane," said Neil, "with the deep voice. I see her around." Now his eyes lit for a moment. "She's looking splendid. On the up and up. Always smiling."

Did he know how I could reach her? "She's around," he said, and paused. "I think she's working at a hostel. The one for recovering alcoholics up in Kemp Town."

I phoned. They told me a Jane, with a different surname, would be in at seven. I left a message and said I would phone again. That voice, deep, conjuring lady wrestlers, vibrant, conjuring Winston Churchill? How did I forget that voice? Gone with Frank's face that I can't even conjure. I had written a short story about my encounter with Jane, and I wanted her to read it. We arranged to met in a pub near her home up at the Seven Dials. She looked her age - late thirties - only a little bit weathered - meeting again after half a life time. Her eyes were still frank, but less transparent then in her wild days. Now she had careful boundaries.

After an exchange of pleasantries, I gave Jane a copy of my story. It being short, she insisted on reading it right there. When she got to the part about stabbing the therapist at the Copenhagen airport, she stopped. "When you phoned yesterday," she told me, "and they said that you had an American accent, I wasn't sure whether it was you or that therapist. I'm glad it was you."

Jane offered some corrections to the story as I had recalled it. It wasn't a knife that she had taken from her handbag at the airport. It was a scissors, though Jane thought that a knife made for a better story. The copy of the story I had given her lacked a title page, and she asked me if the story had a name. "I call it 'Catching Butterflies'," I informed her. "You were the butterfly that I couldn't catch."

Jane explained a few things about our brief interlude - our almost meeting, not quite loving, seventeen years before. "You didn't know I was a lesbian? It pisses my husband off," she said with a tender laugh. Her husband was very ill. Serious T.B. (Or not T.B.) And Crazy Jane took it on the chin. And crazy Jane was sane.

"When I met you I was falling apart again."

"I noticed," I said.

"And after that I fell through the floor. I spent two years on the street. I don't mean whoring. I wasn't up to that. Destitution. Bag lady. Didn't know what time was. What city. Two years sleeping rough. Out of it. Frank Lewis took me in. Saved me. I lived with Frank for two years. I don't mean I lived with him. We were never lovers. I stayed at his place. He looked after me. Amazing man. Almost imperturbable. Finally we had a falling out. A big fight. I guess I had to see if I could move him." She looked wistful. "We patched it up before... He died, you know. In the early eighties. Drove his bike into a wall. I can't help but think that it wasn't an accident. He had cancer. I think maybe..." The words died away.

I told Jane the story of his driving off the road. His hunches. She nodded her head as she listened. And I volunteered the story of the Jade Buddha, the love piece. I don't know why. Jane listened quietly, and then replied, "Then that explains it. When I left, ran away, after we fell out, I took a couple of things from my room. A rug, an ashtray and the Buddha. I'd been with them so long, tender years - I felt they defined... I felt they were mine. Frank called the cops. I could never understand why he did that."

After our brief, not quite affair, Jane had sent me a postcard, a line drawing of God's finger reaching out to Adam as on the ceiling of the Sistine Chapel. "Keep in touch," it said. So here's an answer, seventeen years on, an ode to Spanish Frank; a story, without an ending, unless it's Frank splattered on a wall and my meeting Jane again to find this link between us.

BETSY'S GODDESS

Betsy can see order in the chaos of her room. She adds Bergamot oil to my tea to conjure Earl Grey.

Matthew sees angels enfolding consciousness into our patterned minds. "Enfold" or "condense" are three dimensional words for n-dimensional concepts. The ancients used metaphors to speak to the blind, and wrote do-it-yourself manuals for the willing and able.

Matthew speaks of the "critical mass". There is more consciousness now on the face of the planet...

"That's strange," say I. In a millennium when there was a small fraction of the present population, Lao Tsu, the Buddha and Jesus manifested. Now, in the teeming billions, the Gods are gone.

Betsy says her friend was telling her that all the Goddesses have left: they got into taxis and disappeared into New Jersey. "But," says Betsy, "I saw a woman at the bus-stop yesterday that just needed a word in her ear to manifest her Goddessness. And another in the Laundromat, and two in the café. There are avatars everywhere just waiting a whisper."

SPOONS

BEAR IN THE SEVENTIES:
A DECADE OF PERSONAL GROWTH

My greatest hunger is for a friend. A special friend. I'm looking for that mesh: the excitement of finding someone who can follow my thoughts. Someone who'll be there. Not much to ask. Better than a million dollars. Max Bear was not that friend, but he was as close as I've got, and that shows my poverty.

Long ago in hippy Brighton, nineteen seventy-two, we talked first, Bear and I, in some Steve's house. Max talked of personal growth and Sue Bear bubbled beside him. They drew energy into, drew presence into the dark rooms where some semi-transient Steve hosted Bear to a transient lair. What marked that house? Throw rugs? Pottery? Cushions on the floor! that's it. No couch, no armchairs. Sit on the floor, head tilted back to stare at the mandalas and psychedelic posters, like flags and badges on the walls.

Bear and I went off to a darker room to talk. We crouched down by the foot of a bed, toe to toe, and fountained. I had seen Bear, been introduced, in the weeks before. With an acquaintance I was renting a workshop above Ananda, the local Headshop, where we crafted hardwood pipes - rosewood and exotic woods - each pipe individual. I've never seen pipes as nice again. But it was hardly a living.

Max and Sue Bear had arrived in Brighton chasing Margot, Max's ex, chasing proximity with his first two sons. The two Bears rented a workshop in Ananda to make candles. So I met them first, Max in colourful baggy rags, the holes in the bum that's now so fashionable; Sue in a flowing gown; carrying pots of paint and brushes to paint their work room. "If we're going to work in it, it has got to be a nurturing environment." So Bear, with determination, and Sue Bear, with smiles, painted. Did they actually get round to making candles? I don't recall. So much of the past is shrouded.

Steve's house. Dark room. First real meeting with Bear. What Bear radiated, for me, was excitement. Bear thought life was for voluptuous consumption. Thought life should be delightful, and would be if you grabbed it and played with it. And Bear back then had a mind as sharp as a razor. No. I take that back. As a cutting tool he was woolly. What he had was fireworks. Sparks and crazy lights. Strange illuminations. Wizzbang!

Bear and I went off to talk. And meshed! He understood what I was talking about! And he had more to say on the matter. What matter? Everything!

One of the things Bear spoke of was Kingsley Hall. He had worked in R.D. Laing's famed anti-psychiatric experimental house where kooks, in principle, healed themselves through free flow. In practice it was for the most part free fall. My father rages... (Forgive these asides. My story rambles, like Bear.) My father, Robert, rages that Kingsley Hall was a dud and a fraud. They left his sister, Sarah, to suffer the whims and sins of sadists, he says. Even their one celebrated success, a lady who found herself through paint (worked her way up from shit to oils) later relapsed. "Paranoid exploiters," says Robert and "Marijuana blissed-out creeps, preyed on the crazies," daddy says.

"Hey, Bear never did that."

"Yeah, but he was too stoned to help anyone. Some crazy beat up on Sarah."

"What was Laing doing?"

"Bathing in glory."

What Bear remembered of my aunt, Sarah, and recounted in that first talk, was Sarah being upset with his treatment of his then wife, Matte, and therefore, and there's some crazy logic in it somewhere, she, Sarah, put all Matte's clothes into the bath and shat on them. "Of course it makes sense," says Bear. "She was mirroring my behaviour."

"And did that help anything?"

"We grew, we grew," says Bear.

My next vivid memory is Bear's wedding. A different house. They moved through several squats. The first a basement ruin. Sue Bear then was great with child, so they moved on into a more settled squat, where Sue bore Bear his third son, Ardy, after R.D. Laing. To celebrate Ardy's birth they married. My vivid memory, actually, is of myself sitting under an "orange blossom" tree bearded like Alan Ginsberg. I've got a photo. That's why it stays vivid. My most vivid memory of Bear is of his indifference. He confided in me at the reception that he was dissatisfied with Sue. She wasn't into growth or changes, and sex was getting boring. He was readying to move on. Before then, though, Sue would bare him another son. And first they would move on again together. Move into Joy Corbet's College Terrace "commune".

Was Joy's place a commune? Moot point. Whether it was, or not, the basement apartment that the Bears moved into was self-contained. "We've got stuff to work on."

Actually, anywhere the Bears visited began to feel like a commune. Bear was no respecter of private property. Things vanished from cupboards. Bear was, however, a great respecter of persons, and his appropriations of stuff, borrowings, rarely caused offence. At this period, though, his double standards did raise eyebrows. Joy found his use of her "commune", her space, and the privacy he demanded for the Bear's lair hypocritical. There were other contradictions. Bear gave a series of vocal classes, for non-musicians, and taught us to feel free to sing, to make noise, to vocalise. It certainly freed up my vocal chords, though they're not to this day as free as Bear's. I recall driving with him and Sue to Wales, a year later, to visit my children. In Joy's car. Out of the blue Bear would sing "Allah!" in a clear free voice. "It releases energy." Sure does. I'm still working on it, though, two decades later.

While Bear was freeing up our vocal expression, Joy recalled bitterly how one evening he told Miranda, her twelve year old daughter, not to join in with an awful din on her recorder. "Stifled her," said Joy. "She didn't play that thing again for two years." That's almost as bad as "spoons". Am I going to tell you about spoons? I'll have to meditate on that. "Spoons" is secrets.

Bear brought me "spoons", and Bear brought me meditation. Well, he brought me Rached. Rached was middle-aged, large girthed, white haired and bearded, gay and rather camp. An actor who had some years before gone out to Egypt where he met a sheik who, as far as I can tell, shook him and in turn made him a sheik. I guess that's how it works. One sheik makes another. So now Rached was a Sufi guru. Guardian of the mysteries. Strange, though, to emerge from meditation, from listening to his "psychic" perceptions, and then to watch him bickering with his boyfriend, Kim. To me it made him very non-threatening (the Maharishe's, with their serious pomp, scare me psychically shitless). Rached, just because of his limitations, was no threat to me, and I could use him as a guru. He taught me to sit before the "Beloved". It was Bear who found Rached for us, and through this I owe Bear my introduction into meditation, and the hundreds of hours I've "sat" since..

Bear, Bear, were you there when we stripped the wall paper off Rached's new house and painted and decorated the meditation room? Yes, there you are, down there with the boys, unlike Rached, who would pay for his inactivity (and his diet) soon with heart attacks.

Where to next, Bear? You through several more houses, and another son, the fourth, Flame, and then parting over what issues with Sue. Into phase two.

Bear fell in love. Again and again. And when he wasn't falling in love he was womanizing. He fell in love with Sally, and that took him to London, and brings us back to R.D. Laing, to a second generation of therapeutic households. Laing had set up a Foundation, the Philadelphia Association, which outlived its best known incorporation, Kingsley Hall. It was through the Philadelphia Association that Bear met Sally. Sally ran a house for the association on a Mayfair road, Wood Green, twixt Hackney and Highgate. So Bear moved up to London, or sort of commuted between London and Brighton, between Sally and me. I often felt like his other woman. Abused like his other woman. Though there was never any hint of, you know... Just that as time went on in phase two it felt like he took me more and more for granted.

Bear went up to London town and worked as a busker, a street musician. When he could get out of bed. Bear was a flautist. But his talent was in moving people, in moving "energy". He also had a talent as a lyricist, though this was seldom exercised. He brought me a lyric for my novel, "Pipedreams".

> "They say if you rub two boy scouts together
> You can start a fire
> Bet if we rubbed our souls together
> We could get even higher."

Bear wanted to be a musician, but as a singer and as an instrumentalist he was still a journeyman, and the incongruence in his aspirations led him to doubt his talents, and pulled him towards the grave.

Sally. Sally was an American heiress. Sally drove a Porsche. Not a new one. One of those old beauts. Sally's inheritance came in dribs and drabs. Large dribs and drabs, and Bear helped her spend them. On a trip to Paris, as they sat in a Boulevard Cafe drinking, drinking the day away, Sally agonized about the ruby ring heirloom her mother had given her. A mother of a stone. But Sally felt the ring had bad vibes: death was trapped in the crystal. Blood ruby. "Here, give it to me," said Bear, and he threw it in the trash can. "Shit!" thought Bear. "The waiter may pick it up, someone will end up wearing it, and the bad karma will still be there." So he wrapped it up carefully in a serviette, and again into the trash.

Bear took risks. Bear was a lover. Bear was an explosion of enthusiasms.

"Sally's bosom. I love Sally's bosom. I've never met a woman with such wonderful tits. Not that they're anything to look at, but they're so sensitive. She's so sensuous. Ecstatic tits." (It sounded better in the seventies.)

That was the thing I loved most about Bear: his enthusiasm. He celebrated his friends the way he celebrated Sally's bosom (though that was the only bosom secret of Sally's that he shared with me). Trips to the Mayfair Road house were a delight. Bear lavished the attention on me that I'd craved since infancy. Bear honoured me. Every day was a party. And you, my friend, are invited.

Breakfasts at Mayfair Road were simply toast, bacon, eggs and coffee. That they were, but through Bear's life and gusto they were every day a feast. Then after breakfast there would be our constitutional walk, to the liquor store.

When I first met Bear he had been a polydrugger, not settled on any one poison, and in that somewhat protected from any particular rut. Now, however, he began to focus more and more on booze. Oh, he still did lots of smoke, and memorable mushrooms. I remember Bear "exploding" the garlic into the air into the Mayfair Road kitchen, and a night of hilarity fuelled on 'shrooms. and later, in Brighton, when speed and acid floated us to the beach, I picked up a small piece of driftwood with a delicate pink seaweed ruffled on it. Shoved my nose into it. Smelled the gentle sea. "Here. This is beautiful."

"Botticelli!" screamed Bear.

While Bear commuted between London and Brighton, Sally commuted between London and California. This made for a communications problem. And it accentuated the drinking problem too. Bear's wit addled as a drunk, and drunk he'd cringe and cry. Maudlin beseechings. He on his knees, clawing at me. "I want her! I need her! Why? Why?" Did I fail him? He was so draining. Still the spark would come back, would come through, in fits and starts. Erratic Bear. So many cautionary tales, as for instance that night when I was sharing an apartment with Steve the Creep, when I thought that Steve's estranged wife, who (he claimed) was giving him so much grief about access to his kid, when this Linda was being, it seemed, so cute, so provocative: Bear picked up a small potted cactus and lofted it across Steve's room to splatter on the wall above Steve and Linda. It seemed appropriate. Bear's accidental demolition of the kitchen later that evening seemed less apposite. And later when I found out that this was a different Linda, not Steve's "bitch" wife, the whole evening, in retrospect, lost much of its savour. Steve was tolerant, considering, but it did put a curse on that house-sharing. Still, on the information Bear had it was a creative piece of destruction.

We're walking down the street, past a men's shop. There's a snazzy jacket in the window. Bear goes in to try it on. Pouts and frowns. It isn't him. "Here, you try it on." Italian designer's menswear. Just a beach jacket, but expensive. "It looks great on you. It's yours." I glowed in this demonstration of caring.

Next day my phone bill arrived. Bear had run up five times the cost of his expensive gift phoning Sally in San Francisco. The phone company cut me off, called me in, and put me on an installment pay-off plan.

I still have the jacket Bear bought me. It's rags now, but still my Linus blanket. And eventually Bear did pay the phone bill, though this waited months, awaited his return from San Francisco. Bear's first trip abroad. Oh, the stories he brought. The meeting in a San Francisco bar with the Indian. "Straight spine, clean mind," he said. And the thugs who smashed Bear's hand and his lip, then stole his flute. "You won't be needing that now." Poor Bear on a roll.

The moves from house to house, woman to woman, consumed the years. In the late seventies, there's Bear back in Brighton, driving Sally's Porsche. He's arranging to ship it to her in California. How did I trust him, with no apprehension, to jaunt around with my two young kids piled in there with a bevy of his boys? Was I numb, dumb, or psychic? He crashed the Porsche, of course. No one was damaged, Just some parked car and a thousand pounds worth of Porsche repairs. And when the cops found him they didn't even notice that he was drunk. Just some merry fool.

Then in seventy-nine Bear moved to California chasing

Sally. Sue Bear, an American, coincidently also returned to California. The Bears would both end up in St. Helena, in the Napa Valley above San Francisco. Wine country. And I, too, followed a while later, spending six months in L.A. with my father on my way to Canada and new careers.

Bear was up in St. Helena cause of a guru and because Sally's family mansion was there. Sally, however, checked out, off to New York, no forwarding address. Bear was living with Lucy, a dancer, who was grubbing a living as a car mechanic in St. Helena. Teresa and I drove up to see Bear there. Phase three.

Up rickety cantilevered wooden stairs in the back, back by the tall bamboo grasses, to the walled-in windowed porch adapted as kitchen. California night, St. Helena style. Endless balmy winter's evening. Where's Bear? Danny, a would-be novelist (so many of us) wanders in. "Oh, you're Bear's friend. He'll be here."

Danny's into philosophy. Danny remarks how Bear is the only person he's ever known who could just sit and sweat from frustration.

Bear is working as unskilled labour cleaning up on a house construction. I'd join him at this for a few days. Evenings he is rehearsing for a play. A small amateur local theatre group.

Bear rolls in late, elated to see us, and excited on his own account. "We put on a revue this summer. A sort of free form thing, involving the audience. Singing and dancing. It went over great." Lucy is nursing Bear's fifth son, Joshua. Bear goes to the cupboard. Pulls out Smirnoff and smoke. Old days. Trickle away. There's no room for us to sleep comfortably at Lucy's. Dan's crashing there on the sofa, and the rooms are small. Bear leads us cross town, past midnight, to Sue Bear and Marvino's cottage, to a room with two mattresses, and no light.

Sue and Marvino, Ardy and Flame are driving up from Sue's mother's in Pasadena. They'll be arriving. Don't be alarmed.

My first introduction to Marvino the following morning is a fist clenched hand creeping out from under the bedding on the other mattress. It lifts tentatively into the morning light. Slowly he stretches his little finger, his ring finger. Marvino's morning exercises. Marvino is a clown. He wears a toy bird in his shapeless woollen hat, and shoes sprayed silver. All over St. Helena you'll find the silvered outlines of his feet. Marvino is a clown with a cruel wit. He puts out a newsletter. He doesn't take to me, it seems, for in his newsletter he refers to me as "the novelist's son."

Over breakfast six year old Ardy is acting up. "Eat your pancakes," scolds Marvino. "If you don't behave I'll send you over to your father's and you can have vodka for breakfast."

Bear had a staph infection on this wrist. After our week in St. Helena, when we returned to L.A. I developed a staph infection in the identical spot! Am I close to my friends?

A few weeks later we returned to watch Bear perform. He's playing Bob Cratchett in A Christmas Carol. He's more "theatrical" than the rest of the amateur cast, but there's no great stage presence here. I sense that Bear is looking desperately, last chance, for something meaningful in his life, and I sense his disappointment.

We go out drinking after his performance, and drunk we wander home through the northern California streets. Christmas lights. And I know, and I know we had a poignant exchange, but I'd had too much drink to recall. Did he tell me he loved me? Did he thank me for loving him? Did he explain his life, or mine? Did he tell me he felt my frustration at genius not attained, his and mine? Did he berate me for some betrayal? Did he tell me about spoons? No, that was much earlier, in Brighton, and here comes the betrayal.

Spoons is our code for darkest secrets told in confidence, to be kept for ever. When Max Bear was younger, pre-Bear, still working in advertising but shifting into hippy gear, he shared a kitchen with, among others, a woman with a two year old child. The child was quite wild, and quite a pain. One day it was banging a wooden spoon on its highchair. Max started banging the kid on the head with the wooden spoon. Max was horrified as he observed himself. It was this incident that told him that he needed to change.

I don't think it was spoons, or the like, that pulled Bear apart. I think it was his appreciation of fine things, and his wish to create them with talents he then lacked. His talent was as a catalyst, and he had scant respect for his talent. And alcohol was easier for him than diligence or patience.

We all have our spoons. Mine include that I spill them, spill spoons, but only after years have passed, and with love.

Bear loved California. "Do you know, there's thirty-three percent spirit in Vanilla essence, and you can get it in the all night supermarket."

The last I heard of Bear he was arrested for shoplifting Vanilla essence in the Napa A & P.

CODA: Spilling Bear's spoons is one of the most drastic things I've ever done, as bad as spoons itself. All I can say* is that it was a decade later, and I didn't think that Bear had survived, or perhaps that in a twisted way I didn't think he had survived as a human being.

Then 34 years after I'd last seen Bear I got an email: "Bear is alive and well and living in San Antonio. Botticelli!" OMG

Bear's life went up and down generally progressing towards healing. Bear has trained as a counselor, works in addiction treatment, deeply involved in Buddhism, continuing to play and master the flute.

In return to my WOW answering email, Bear writes, "Haven't told ANYONE about spoons since you. So you're a scumbucket for blowing it! I actually don't have any anger at all about it. Still feel bad about doing it. I CAN report however that

---

* 2015: decades later: the *"past life"* story might explain my need to spill Bear's spoons (see: Norman Allan: the story for Ezra, book two, chapter two at http://www.normanallan.com/Lit/NA%20the%20story/B2%20 Chpt%202.htm). Just an excuse and an explanation.

it's STILL the worst thing I ever did in 67 years. My main sins have been of omission. Absentee father; the worst consequence of my alcoholism by far.

"Next to your email (writes Bear) was one from my fifth son, David - of whom you won't have heard, right? Suffice it to say he signed off with 'l love you very much, Dad.' So it ain't all bad

on my cosmic scoreboard. David is a 34 year old artist (painting & sculpture) and lives in California with his wife Jean and their six year old son Joseph. Who's a mensch!"

Spilling spoons? I feel very unclear about the propriety of this. If any one does see it, who knows Bear, well, I can rationalize that as part of the (universal) restitution, as far as Bear is concerned. As for me, well that's a long story…

THE MAYAN CREATION MYTH:
WHY THINGS ARE AS THEY ARE

Nando sat on his futon in front of his laptop. "I'm writing about the Mayan story of creation." Nando is a Mayan medicine man. He's been my house guest these many months.

It seems there was a counsel of Creators.

"Like a committee?" I asked.

"Like a circle," said Nando.

In the beginning this committee, this circle of Creators made creatures out of wood, but the wooden men neglected to give due respect to the Creators, so they burned them. Then the Creators made men out of mud, out of clay, but again, they clay creatures failed in this respect, so the Creators washed them away.

"Ah ha!" I said. "That explains why the world is such a mess. The Creators were a bunch of bumblers."

"No," said Nando (with a heavy accent). "It all works out fine. Next the Creators created the animals, and that was good, and though the animals didn't give much attention to the creators, there was no blame in that. So next the Creators made men, and women. But then they thought, the people are a little too clever. 'Ah ha. They are clever like us,' so the Creators took away men's vision, their inner vision - they closed the third eye - and they took away their patience."

"Just the men?" I said.

"Just the men," said Nando.

"Well, indeed, that does explain a lot. They are not very kind, the Creators."

"Oh no," said Nando. "They gave us dreams."

CODA: Not to worry too much. When the Mayan calendar renews in 2012, I believe that many of us are due to get our vision and our patience back, and live in reality rather then the dream world.

The story Hamach *forms most of chapter one of* Norman Allan: the story, for Ezra, *which is posted on line*, but which I'm unlikely to "publish" (I've borrowed so many images for* NA:tsfE, *I'd need an intern to sort that out. So we'll publish it here.*

(If you go on to read Norman Allan: the story, for Ezra, *or have read it, you might want to skip reading* Hamach *twice.)*

* *Norman Allan: the story, for Ezra: book one, chapter one,* Hamach at www.normanallan.com (http://www.normanallan.com/Lit/NA%20the%20story/NAts%20Chpt%201.htm#chpt1)

HAMACH

Let me tell you of my meeting with Hamach and his prediction of the hour of my death. It's a rambling tale that winds through Chauffeur Mike.

The second time I met Mike the Chauffeur was up on Cissbury Tor. And that was moments after my meeting with Crazy Jane. It led me to Marrakech, to Hamach. The first meeting with Mike the Chauffeur had been a year before at a "squat" in Brighton. Alan Dare, of the Open Café, asked me to photo-document the squat so the police couldn't say the squatters had trashed the place. But they did. They trashed the place down to the legendary piano for fire wood.

Why was he "Mike the Chauffeur"? Because, he said, he had driven the getaway car.

Up at the concert on the Downs, leaving beaming Jane with an understanding that we would be in touch, I turned and walked towards the music, towards the stage. I think the mushrooms were beginning to bite, the fly agaric from Viking Nick.

To my left, as I walked across a small glade, was a lean-to hut of branches and polythene. Outside it stood a small group of deadbeat "heads", Mike among them. (We hippys, we called ourselves "heads", or "freaks". "Ah, you're nay freaks," said the young Scot in Covent Gardens.) Up on Cissbury Tor, Mike the Chauffeur recognized and greeted me and told me that everything was simply wonderful with him. He'd been travelling. He was in business - very successful. He had an apartment in Rome and an apartment in Marrakech.

"Marrakech?" I echoed. I was writing my first novel, a hippy fairy tale, Pipedreams, which was set, in part, in Morocco, in the Riff. I never got to the Riff - I let a hipster in Casablanca part me from my money - but Marrakech? Well, I was ready to travel; explore; new life; possibly to Canada, to look up Linda, to inquire after Bren. But perhaps Marrakech first, for the sake of the novel. "Ahm," said Mike. "I've, er, left this girl looking after the place, English girl, Helen McDuff. Ah, what the hell, just tell her I said you could stay. Stay as long as you like." And he scribbled the address for me on a little scrap of paper: 1 Rue Mohammed Cinque.

Now this was a gift horse worth a look in the mouth, but a short while later I bumped into Viking Nick, who had organized this little free festival, the concert up on the Tor. I spoke to Nick of my encounter with the "chauffeur", of his flat in Marrakech and that I might travel. "Helen, yeah. I know her," he said. "Tall blond girl. Ex-mate of my mate Brent. She stayed on out in Marrakech when they split up. Everybody there knows her. The Moroccans call her Aisha, because of her blond hair." So the address seemed legitimate. I had a place to stay in Marrakech and a few weeks later, after my brief butterfly affair with Jane, I set out.

As I mentioned above, I let a Moroccan hipster talk me out of my money in Casa - a long story. I hitchhiked to Marrakech to find that the Rue Mohammed Cinque is the main street in the new French city. One Rue Mohammed Cinque is the address of the main mosque, the Katubia. Oops.

Homeless and near penniless I wandered into the main square, the Jamal F'na. There were rows and rows of booths filling most of the square: baby "souks". (A souk is a shop and "the souk" is the market.) One of the awninged kiosk shops had a hippy flare. Several longhairs were sitting there with the young proprietor. Standing outside it in the North African sun, I inquired after the blond McDuff. The proprietor shook his head, he didn't know, and then beckoned me, inviting me in to sit and drink mint tea and smoke kif with them, in the Moroccan pipe, the sebi.

Speaking passing English, the proprietor, Hassan, made me welcome. The cool, the hip, stopped and gossiped in his stall as they passed from the old town, the Medina, to the new city through the square, the Jamal F'na. Of each new arrival I inquired after Aisha, after McDuff. Hours passed. Hassan and God, Allah, were patient with me.

Then a tall, superhip, young Moroccan stopped with us a while, another Hassan. There are incredible numbers of Hassans and Mohammeds in Morocco. (What made this Hassan "superhip"? He was relaxed, completely at home in his skin.)

"Perhaps I can help you," said superhip young Hassan. "Meet me tomorrow, at four."

Hassan, the shop keeper, directed me to a cheep, honest, "hotel" where for a small price I got a small, bare room and a rush mat for the night. There was no lock on the door. I stood a litre coca cola bottle, in which I had water for the night, behind the door, to fall and clatter if anyone opened the door (as would Chris Pasha, the hero of my hippy-tale, Pipedreams). No one disturbed us.

Hip Hassan's friend was, indeed, Helen, but she was not actually called Helen McDuff. She McDonaugh. And Helen did not know remember Mike the Chauffeur. "He must have crashed in the pad sometime, but I don't recall him." And further, she had lost her apartment a few days before (I don't recall the circumstances). She was staying with friends. But she took pity on me. "Wait here. I will make some inquiries." An hour later she returned with a solution.

Helen's friend, Nicole, put me up. The hippy-go-lucky seventies were sure different days. Can you imagine taking in a stranger today? (Then you are probably some latter-day hippy.)

Nicole was a colleague of Helen's, a teacher at the English school. She was older, but with a young mien. Her teenage daughter, a student at the school, helped to tie her to the younger set. She lived in a bungalow, by no means small, in the new city. And there I was ensconced for a week or ten days till Helen found and rented a house in the Medina.

Nicole was having an affair with one of her students, Nasari. Why mention this? Nasari's friend, Yves, will figure in our story, in a moment.

What else to tell of Marrakech? That it was hot? Forty degree, a dry oven. That I was in culture shocked, you bet, beset with beggars every time I ventured abroad till, perhaps ten days after I arrived, I went the campground and sat and smoked with English and Dutch and French heads, some moments in a familiar European enclave, and that settled me. I arrived. After that, having recovered from "culture shock", I no longer attracted beggars, would-be-guides, and kids, like flies. I acquired acquaintances and friends.

Oh, and the money. I had read that Anthony Quinn was in Marrakech shooting Mohammed. My father had worked with Quinn. I wrote Quinn a cheque for a hundred dollars. "I my not cash this,"he said. But he did.

I should find another space to tell you of Aram and Azezza, but here I would say this. Before I had settled, while still in culture shock, I had visited them in their house deep in the Medina and spoke of feeling lost. Aram said, "Wherever you sit, that is your space."

And I should speak of Etienne, and Etienne's garden...

And of course I should speak of the musicians in the Jamal F'na, the Gnawa people, dark skinned from the south, with their three stringed bass, the gimbi. The Gnawa musician would sing and thump out a powerful music, while a friend would clack the metal clackers and dance. A circle 'd formed round them. How honored I felt when I was invited into the musician's space, to sit in their inner circle in the hot North African timeless night.

And so the weeks passed.

"Etienne is having a party," said Helen. "He told me to invite you."

The party in Etienne's garden was a farewell-bash for Teresa. Teresa was blond and young. She had a beautiful, noble face. She walked with a crutches. "Polio" she said. She had spent her teens in Marrakech - she was the princess of Marrakech - and now she was returning home, next week, towards Poland.

"When can I meet you again," I asked.

"Here in Etienne's garden. Come tomorrow at noon."

We spent the next afternoon and evening together and meet the next day again and the next. Teresa invited me to travel with her to Avingon where she would spend a month at the Avingon Festival, on her way home to Poland. We arranged to meet in Paris a week hence.

On my way home to Helen's house in the Medina that night, I stopped for a moment in a souk. A real souk, not the kiosk in the square. As you left the square and entered the Medina, the old city, the first shop you'd come across belonged to another Mohammed and Hassan. I've written of them in a short story, The Lady with the Boots. I'll not speak of them further here, just to say that they suggested I go back deep into the shop and met their country cousin. Perhaps he was rolling up.

Deep, deep in back of the souk was a simple young man entertaining two local teenage girls dressed in jeans, tees, running shoes, each with can of coke in hand. The young man was slim, mid-twenties, nothing remarkable about him. He sported relatively short, curly, dark hair, and again, jeans, tee-shirt.

"I'm Norman," I said, or was I Pasha then? I was Pasha quite a while in the seventies. Whoever I was, the poor country cousin, in answer, started to mirror me, each twitch of the eyebrow, each quiver of the jaw. That's a very challenging thing, to be mirrored anywhere, but particularly by a stranger and in a foreign country. And it went on and on, well, not an eternity, but a thorough test, before he broke off from mirroring and, in stilted English, said, "We are brothers. You call me Hamach. Don't use this word with stranger. Is bad word. Hamach mean crazy. But we are brothers, friends. You call me Hamach." He paused, then said, "Give me your hand," and before I could offer, he took it.

Hamach studied my palm for a moment and, pointing to the small calluses, he said, "There is much money."

Now, it's no great thing to be told by a poor Moroccan that you are, or will be, rich, for indeed, relative to the third world poor, we are fabulously wealthy, so I was not impressed with much money. "How much life is there," I asked.

Without hesitation he answered, "Thirty years, one month, one day, two hours."

I thought a moment, calculated: Wow! If he was one year out, mistakenly rounding it a thirty, instead of thirty one, then that would make this very moment exactly the half way point in my life!

Then Hamach took a piece of string from his pocket. He measured the collective length of my left fingers and compared it to my forearm. "Love will not go well," he said.

I told him that my marriage had come apart. "That is good," he said, and took my other hand. Again he compared the finger length against the forearm, and beamed. "There is a woman who loves you bazzef." (Bazzef is one of those first words that one first learns in a foreign tongue - beaucoup, mucho, bazzef.) Then his face clouded. "There is someone who watches you. He is not big, not little. He watches and he is very jealous." And it was this jealous, envious watcher that most impressed itself on Hamach. He returned to it three or four times emphatically. He also returned with enthusiasm, to the woman who loved me bazzef - and this right after Teresa had invited me to travel to Avingon - but he returned again and again to stress the one who watched with envy.

I left the shop around ten o'clock and stepped out right into Helen McDonaugh's path as she walked past from the Medina towards the square. "I was looking for you," she said. "We need to talk."

We went to a café on the Jamal F'na. "Yves going to rent a room from me. He's paid me the rent and he's moving in tomorrow. And he wants you to leave."

I spent my last few nights in Marrakech back at Nicole's. As you might guess, I was greatly impressed with Hamach's reading. He saw my failed marriage. He saw Teresa's love. (Teresa was a classmate and a close friend of Nicole's daughter and, in that, part of Nasari and Yves' circle.) But he saw loudest the event I would walk into from his reading: Yves envy. How could I doubt that he could also see my death: that I would die this coming August, August sixth, 2005.

A while ago I was round at Teresa's for her fiftieth birthday. We've been separated - divorced - for years and years, but we're closest of friends. In some context, that evening, I started talking about Charles Darwin and I put Darwin on the Bounty! "The Beagle." Lynn, a mutual fiend, corrected.

Then, a little later, I spoke to Lynn about my perception of Teresa and my cat, Sativa's, behaviour when we broke up. "No, it wasn't like that," said Teresa. (I've written about this in a short sketch, Cat's Home.) And that got me thinking how I have now and again, and again, misperceived the world. And all of a sudden, after thirty years, I was back in that souk in Marrakech asking, "How much life is there?"

"Thirty(one) years, a month, a day, and two hours," Hamach said, and that was precisely, to the minute, the amount of time I had lived up until then. "How much life...?," I had asked, and he answered telling me how long I had lived.

I WAS TOO DISTRACTED
(Migwetch Here-ra:
Speaking in Tongues)

I've been looking to go home. The sage said look to the heart, the route to the ineffable, the way home. How difficult could that be?

When I was a lad we moved cross the great Atlantic to a strange city. There we rented a home that came with a cat.

Pooh Cat, to look at, was an unprepossessing cat: a feisty tabby. She would sit on the brick pedestal that housed the front gate and dangle her paw to tempt taunt or claw passing dogs. She once chased a friend's spaniel yelping round the yard till rescued.

Pooh Cat became a friend. I seem to draw them. Not friends: cats.

Pooh was eleven or twelve, my age.

One day coming home I found a lump or bundle in my bed, beneath the blanket, that purred when touched: Pooh and kittens.

Before that, though, I think it was I found the cat curled up sleeping in the closet, and I went and snuggled my face, my nose, into her belly. And that was my first experience of true intimacy.

And have I had any since? Oh, degrees. But even when you said I love you, I was distracted.

There's something else I want to mention some absolute meaning that's supposedly in Sanskrit chants. We know that words are symbols and don't have meaning in themselves. But the Sanskrit bit, that here there is power and meaning in the sound itself,

OM Sat Chit Ananda, the very breath of God.

So I was a little in an altered state the other day but focused
and here, somewhat present, and saying goodbye to my dog
Lucky, going out… at the door, but I stopped and crossed the
room to put my face to Lucky's side, and paused, and Proust
back to Pooh Cat   a life ago   oh grace

Migwetch, Here-ra, I said.

Migwetch is "thank you" in Annishnabi, the language of this
land where I live.
Here-ra. Here-ra is a neologism: a slur of heart and *hridya*,
heart in Sanskrit. *Here-ra* is a private name I've called my dog.

Migwetch Here-ra, I said to Lucky, talking in tongues.

THE SINGING OF A PATRIOTIC SONG

On my first trip to Ireland in 1972 I took with me a romance. Knowing of the "singing pubs" where everyone is invited to do a turn, to sing a song or recite a poem, I determined to sing "Kevin Barry" - a patriotic song.

I hitchhiked across the waist of the wee country. In one town, halfway between Dublin and Limerick, I was picked up on the way into town and driven the half mile to the other side. During our few minutes together I confessed to my hosts, two rough country diamonds, of my ambition to sing Kevin Barry in a pub. Now this was during the time of the troubles in Ulster - when was it not? - and in this context the driver turned at his wheel to face me and my English accent. "I wouldn't be doing that," he said. "It could be dangerous."

Early on a Friday morning
High upon a gallows tree
Kevin Barry gave his young life
For the cause of liberty

I hitched on to County Clare on the west coast, and walked the carless countryside. On a winding road through a hospitable valley I stopped to watch a young man placing stones in a wall. In a while he stopped to chat, and soon invited me into the farm cottage for the ubiquitous boiled egg. The young man and his father owned seventeen cows, but served me Blue Band Margarine, and Wonderloaf, and Hartley's jam, and Tetley's tea. Tate and Lyle sugar. All brand names, save for the milk and the egg. The cottages have open hearths for a small peat fire. There is a "crane" from which to hang pots over the fire. And that's the kitchen. No running water. My host and his portly father -

bursting shirt, worn tweed jacket - warmed the batteries of their tiny transistor radio by the ashes and embers to eke out another few minutes of current and transmission.

After spending a few days with some friends in County Clare, I hitched down to Kerry where I stayed a short spell with another friend, Jonathan Clark, who was holidaying in Kerry with his beautiful wife, Kate. There were two guests there before me; two "lads" from Belfast, Provisional IRA, active urban guerrillas, on a rest and respite. Michael was in his mid twenties and was a gentle, thoughtful lad. While we others talked, ate, drank, and smoked dope, he sat by the fire reading James Joyce's Ulysses.

"Michael," I asked, "are you familiar with a passage that goes something like "a woman no better than something..."

Michael, who was half way through the thousand page text, turned back one page to read, "Helen, a woman no better than she should be..." Helen as in Helen of Troy.[1]

Michael's comrade, Sean, was a harder study. Now in his mid thirties, Sean had been a shop steward, an activist even before the troubles moved his activities underground. He was a political man, a rationalist, pragmatist, cutting through problems with little display of emotion.

Just a lad of eighteen summers
But there's no one can deny
As he waked to death that morning
Kevin held his head up high.

My second day in Kerry, Matt Murphy and American Debbie, his young plump blond hippie sleep-in, came to visit. Matt Murphy, now sixty, thin, greying slicked hair, grown reedy from Guinness and whisky, Matt Murphy had been a drinking companion of Brenden Behan, the Dublin playwright. Behan

---

[1]"Helen, a woman no better than she should be", occurs near the beginning and again halfway-ish.

and Murphy had decided one evening that what Ireland needed was for some hero with the balls and wit to walk stark naked down O'Connell Street. I do not know whether Ireland as a whole noticed, remembers, or thanked them, but for the cognoscenti it rendered Murphy some notoriety. At the time I met him, Matt Murphy, down in Kerry, was famous again, not only as the late playwright's buddy, but also for his cowboy boots, hat, and belt. But then all the Irish are famous for one thing or another. By this time Behan had drunk himself into his grave. Matt Murphy, himself, was working on it. But despite his pallor (and you could see through him on a bright day), there was still one foot out of the grave. Murphy talked of old times and drank whatever was in the house.

Another martyr for old Ireland
Another murder for the crown

After our meeting with Matt Murphy, the Belfast lads were planning to drive back to Dublin. I begged a ride. Sean was planning to leave at two in the morning - this in order to arrive at Matt Murphy's, on the tip of the Kerry peninsula, at three a.m. As we drove in our stolen Ford Escort I learnt of the purpose of our visit. Matt Murphy owned a gun. An old rifle. A memento of the First Great War. It had seen service during the Rebellion. And Murphy had inherited it from an uncle. "So it's a very old gun, but it is serviceable," said Sean. The Provisional needed every weapon they could lay their hands on. "He calls himself a patriot. Now we'll see - if he'll give us the gun. It's all fine words."

We arrived at an old two story house in the unwatched hours. We knocked and knocked and called, quietly but insistent. "Murphy, be Jesus. Wake yourself, man. Your country's calling."

Debbie, the plumb little hippie dumpling, tousle-headed, but not unfriendly, opened the door. Murphy was asleep, deep with pills.

"Rouse him. We've business."

Groggy Matt Murphy stumbled downs stairs and entered the room, rumpled but unruffled. "Jesus, man. I've taken a whole pharmacy. I can't be awake."

"We've come for the gun."

"The devil you have."

"Is it here?"

"It's buried where it will do no harm. In the hills. I'll nar givit ya."

They haggled. "Your country..."

"My arse..."

Finally Murphy yawned and stretched. "Look, man, I'm asleep." It was a hard statement to contest for he was indeed all but sleeping, and he was adamant. A winning combination. Debbie and I, half in, half out of the picture, observed the midnight farce with apprehension. Might there be violence? No, there would not, but the boys would grumble a lot, Sean anyroad, all the way to Dublin.

"Calls himself a patriot!"

We drove to Killarney, arriving at four in the morning. "We'll have to wait till six for petrol." An anticlimax, three men kipping in a Ford Escort in the forecourt of the petrol station on the outskirts of Killarney.

And then a wild drive to Dublin. Seventy and eighty miles an hour on those Irish roads is wild enough. Always the crows busy by the edge of the road.

It came my time to drive. The Belfast boys in the back were discussing stratagems to change the fate of nations. The English just wanted them to roll over and play dead, opined Sean, but he wasn't about to oblige them. "You know, thirty dedicated men can tie down fifteen thousand English troops in Ulster. Indefinitely. They'll tire of it before we do. They can't afford it."

So there I was, boys, chauffeuring the Belfast lads in their stolen car. I felt like James Dean. And I asked if I might sing for them as I drove our rebel wagon. "Right enough," said Michael. "On you go," said Sean.

Shoot me like an Irish soldier
Do not hang me like a dog
For I fought for Ireland's freedom
On that cold September morn
All around that little bakery
Where we battled hand to hand
Shoot me like and Irish soldier
For I fought to free Ireland.

BROKEN TULIPS

I was standing with my mother and my children in Brighton's central "square", the Olde Steine. There had been a storm the night before and three year old Seth asked if he could step over the small fence to pick out the broken stemmed tulips in the bed that ringed the fountain. "Sure," I said, and five years old Jessi joined him. Mother and I stood talking.

Mother must have been disappointed in her dropped-out divorced son. Me a would be writer, writer like her ex who'd walked out. She was certainly disappointed in my long hippie hair. (This is the nineteen seventies.) For years the first thing she would say when we met was, "When are you going to get your hair cut?"

"When are you going to get your hair cut?" I did not get on with my mother.

My new girl friend was handicapped. "You'll have to take taxis."

We talked.

As we talked we were approached by an old lady (with another old lady and an elderly gentleman in tow). The old biddy came up to us, ignored my mother and I, and addressed my young children. "Your father should have told you not to pick the flowers," she said.

I was stunned.

I roared. Like a lion. "Arrrhh!"

The little old lady froze. Extended moments. At least a second or two.

I twitched, bobbed my head forward. The little old lady ran.

My mother made no comment. I would speculate that she was both shocked and proud... proud that we were the alpha lions on the square. (Is that young man's, an immature young man's thought?) Proud that I would defend my children? More shocked than proud. I guess.

The fact that she made no comment, though, made a big impression on me. It wiped out all those years of "When are you going to get your hair cut?"

A couple of hours latter, we were walking down to the station - Mommy was going back up to London - and she did ask, quietly, if I thought I needed any (psychotherapeutic) help.
    Well, nobody's perfect.

OOBI

Ron Hellman was close to being the man that I wanted to be. That's how I saw him when I met him. If I had had Tee's perspicacity I would have know better. His last sortie would not have surprised me.

In 1978, fifty-six years old Hellman's youthful vigour belied his snow white curls. A clean shaven Santa Claus on a bicycle, thin, and seen all over town: who is on his crossbar? where are his hands? In the air, "Look Ma! Ho ho ho". That's how I see him. Playboy of the Low Lands. In denim. Tee reminds me, we... he found this long cardboard carton roll, twenty foot long by the road side. Strapped it on to our little yellow Fiat, like a tank, proboscis proceeding. Tee, though lame, rode gamely home on Ron's cross-bar. Through cobbled streets. Was it a thrill? You bet. Just for the adventure.

Hellman lived in a studio apartment. Wood panels lent the room warmth. A wall of windows afforded a panorama - one could see the river from anywhere in the room - and they placed one, these windows, right in the heart of time, right in the heart of now. Now was Dortdrect. I'd never heard of Dortdrect. It's one of the older cities of Holland, bordered by river, laced by canals.

Ronald Hellman was Steve the Creep's friend. We stopped, unannounced, on our drive across Europe from Poland. Tee's baby Fiat crammed with all her belongings. (Do Fiats have gills?) Despite the Netherland's reputation, there are some long hills.

The little car had begun to complain, and it was a welcome haven to be with Hellman. Ron with his white hair and his occasional son. His wife lived crosstown, and painted. Holland loves painters. Everyone clothes themselves with culture. Anyone willing to put up with the privation of an artist's subsistence can find a grant, or at least a welfare cheque, and just as important, with it comes a public indulgence, if not quite applause and approval. The artist community thrives, and to some extent, so do the arts.

Ron and Hilda Hellman left a relatively affluent existence in Greenwich Village, driven, I believe, by "alienation" - now there's a word - driven by isolation to the refuge of the old world. Warmth, that's Europe as I romanticise her now after ten years wandering in the wastelands of the new world. Ron and Hilda left the desert of MacDonald and Coca Cola dunes for rebirth in the old lands, low lands. They settled, but soon parted, in Dortdrect, and shuffled their child, Ron junior, at thirteen years old a gangly lad, awkward in his growth-spurt years. He sat morosely in the corner our first night there. Then disappeared. "Why has the kid got a chip that big on his shoulder with a father like that?" I wondered. I'd learn.

Ronald senior was a man of several parts. His current passion was designing clocks. Bizarre clock faces. Metal model fish swimming through a cloud-puffed sky to indicate the time. Or shoelaces pointing round a worn-out sneaker.

Clocks were Ron's passion, but games were his living. He'd left the bosom of advertising fifteen years before to pilot the waters of invention, creating games and toys. You won't have heard of any of his board games. They float a hundred "Wall Street This" and "Madison Avenue That"s to come up with one "Monopoly". You may, however, have heard of one of his toys. Ron was the inventor of the Oobi. "Oo" as in "do" and "shubeedoobeedo".

Oobi was a clam-like piece of orange-red plastic, three inches by two and a half inches in diameter and about an inch tall, with two big eyes printed on. Amused eyes. Soulful eyes. There was also a message printed. "Hi! I'm Oobi. I'm going to visit..." and a blank to fill in a name and address. The idea was that, say you're living in New Jersey and you've got a friend in Oregon, and you've sent them letters, and you've talked on the phone, but they're still three thousand miles away. Well, you buy an Oobi, and you put a message in - Oobi was hollow, with a slot. You wrote on the outside, I'm going to visit "Joyce at

1000 Washington Street, Portland, Oregon", or whatever. Then you leave the Oobi in a public place somewhere, a dinner counter, a washroom, and somebody picks it up. "Hey, I'm going in that direction." So Oobi hitch-hikes from counter to counter: encounter to encounter.

Oobi was a child of the sixties, connecting people with goodwill. That's an idea that sold stuff in the sixties. It certainly sold songs. And it sold Ron's creation to a big toy conglomerate who spent several million dollars manufacturing and marketing Oobi. But Oobi didn't fly. And Ron Hellman, father of Oobi, like most of my readers, had never had his day brightened by a message passed from hand to hand: "Hi! I'm Oobi!" So Oobi died. Ron had just two surviving Oobis left. He gave us one. It was quite an honour to receive the penultimate Oobi.

Now Ron, besides his clocks, was designing video war games. Time moves on.

Tee recalls Ronald's comment that you could judge the size of a man's cock by his confidence, and the quality of a woman's cunt by the shape of her mouth. It put her back up. Ron stared at women's faces in a disquieting way.

Tee recalls Ronald being offended that she should make a suggestion on how he might finish one of the clock faces, the face then in progress. It put his back up. Tee recalls that I took his part. It put a space between us. Perhaps that space is still there. How do we bridge it? "Hey, don't tell me how to finish my story." It's fifteen years on. My confidence has grown. Has her mouth grown fuller or thinner? Just kidding.

Ron had a friend in Philadelphia, Martin, a cartoonist, and they exchanged letters. Special letters. An exercise in literature and illustration. Illuminated letters. Treasures. Martin's manuscripts were fit for a museum. Ron, recipient of this trove, showed off his archive with the pride and enthusiasm of a child. Tee recalls that Ronald had a disdain for mediocrity. In his manner of living, his panache, and more particularly in his correspondence, Ronald felt that he was a king. The thick brown binder, with its epistolary wealth, was a king's ransom. There was a philosophy that went with this about how friends could enrich and ennoble one another.

We didn't get to see the letters Ron sent to Martin. He confided that they weren't the jewels that he received. He lacked Martin's illustrative flare and genius, but he was proud of the prowess of his prose. He sent studied letters, painstakingly contrived.

Despite the friction between Tee and Ron, those two days in Dortdrect warmed my heart. I glowed in Ron's attention. He shepherded us round town to meet artists galore, to smoke dope in pubs, in public, no fear of bust or stigma. Paranoia gone. A gentler, kinder civilization. Santa Ron cycled round the town, white locks waving in the wind. Greeting every town dog by name. Stopping to converse with children in pigeon Dutch and pigeon English.

I idealised him. Delighted in this middle-aged man who knew how to live. Playfully, with culture at his shoulder. This meeting seemed to promise me that my life, too, could be passionate, without compromise.

Not long after we returned to England, with Tee now living with me, we moved out of the flat I had shared with Ronald's friend, Steve. I sent Ron our new address. Daunted by his and Martin's exalted correspondence, I filled the page with repetitive drivel: "I don't know what to write so I'll just write I don't know what to write so I'll just write..." The new address neatly copied in the top right-hand corner.

A week later a letter arrived from the Netherlands with two tiny slips of paper inside. One, cut off the right-hand corner of my letter, was our address returned to sender, as it were. The other, the left hand corner of my letter snipped off, and on this Ron wrote a terse two word message. "How stupid!" it said.

The penultimate Oobi was sitting on a shelf in the bathroom. His soulful eyes had warmed me in those weeks he'd been with me. His orange-red plastic presence [he spoke of "friendship" to me] his presence actually seemed to glow. Now he would soothe my wound. I put him in a box, and sent him through the regular channels, the post, the mail, not risking him to the hazards of the hitch-hiking life he was contrived for. I sent him surely back to Ron, so Ron might one time get to open an Oobi. A little slip of paper tucked inside. "How sad," it read.

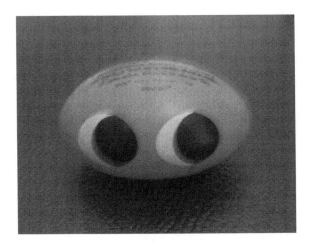

There is an Oobi website
http://www.deuceofclubs.com/oobi

JEWISH NUMBERS AND THE "N" WORD

Slavko has been having bad luck. The decades have cascaded on him. Now, in his seventieth year, he dreamed of lottery numbers. He became vividly alert and he remembered the numbers when he woke. He told me, and he knows I'm Jewish, has a high regard for me, but he has the habit of identifying any Jewish person he interacts with as "Jewish this" and "Jew that"... in the manner of how our dear white Christian brothers might identify, say, a *black* lawyer..." or an "*Indian* doctors, or a Jew...

When my father was a lad in the 1920s, 1930s, he followed his mad dad as he raved on a Montreal streetcar ranting, "We're not the Jews. The Negroes they're the Jews."

So Slavko told me, "The 7 and the 9 were good, but the 13, that was a Jewish number, so I changed it." He changed the 13 to an auspicious number (I forget which) and there was another Jewish number, but all the numbers he dreamed, Jewish numbers and all, were good. He won a hundred dollars for getting four numbers right but missed out on the ten million dollar jackpot that the Jewish numbers might have brought him. It preyed on him for weeks. And then after that other, normal misfortunes resumed and continued to rain on him.

VIE AND THE
SUSSEX STUDENTS' STRIKE

I have wanted to write about Vie and about the Sussex University Paint Throwing incident for some time. I have thought that together they would tell a story about passion and action and change. I believe that all well meaning people want change, yet political action often seems to change very little, where passion can change your life. The link that ties Vie and the paint throwing incident together is Gary, but when we have a woman of Vie's proportions she may tend to take centre stage and others may be ignored, or at least upstaged. The men might be left to play their games like Vietnam, or the Paint Incident.

Now Vie was as big as the sky. I think she invented the "New Age"; invented it and then left it for Punk. When I met her she wasn't yet Vie. She was Frances. She was giving a workshop on bodywork, imaging and such, in the crypt above Rached's café. "Tell Pasha about the Body Show," said Gary.

"The Body Show is a group of students who want to take a revue up to the Edinburgh Festival. They've done a couple of shows, so they think that they are experts. But they want to include some Townies," said Frances.

"A sociology project," said Gary.

"For our verve and piazzas," said Frances. Frances was from London and from culture. She was alive. She had been a potter, quite successful, living in the country, big house, married to a lawyer… but that palled. She took Gary's "Creative Engagement" course. At the end of the semester she left her kiln and husband and moved down to Brighton with Gary. Gary came from Coventry where they used to make cars. Gary lectured in sociology at the London Polytechnic, so now he commuted to town on the Brighton Belle. "The Pullman cars of the Brighton Belle have finally pulled me out of the working class," said Gary. Later, when they phased out the Belle, Gary phased out of his job.

Among Frances's first projects in Brighton was an attempt to start a Community Centre. For two years that was unpaid paperwork and proposals and meetings. And meanwhile there were workshops, and the Body Show.

Frances and Gary and I became fast friends. I read them my fantasy, "Pipedreams", as I wrote it. And we worked out the problems of the universe. Frances thought the problem was that we were caught in nineteen sixty eight and couldn't escape into the mid-seventies. "We have to look forward." So we worked on the Body Show.

What was the Body Show? We didn't know. But it <u>would</u> manifest. We intended that it would highlight mind-body dualism and, with a little bit of luck, abolish it. We dreamed it would be "deep". We hoped that it would be fun. We were determined that it would be entertaining, and informative.

"If the show is going to have any value," said Frances, "we will have to achieve an intimate sincerity."

"And a sincere intimacy," said Gary.

"We will have to overcome all our resistances. Where are the blocks between us, within us? What pertinent truth you would rather not tell me? Ah, there is something, Pasha. You looked away."

"I'm not sure it's relevant," I hedged, but it was. "I suppose the one thing I've avoided saying that is pertinent to the Body Show is that I don't find large women a turn on."

Frances seemed to take this in her stride, never batted an eye. "Oh," she said, "and I thought all this time that you were coming on to me." Then she must have brooded. At the next rehearsal she presented us with a song, The Kitchen Floor Stomp. "I'm cleaning up all trace of you from off my kitchen floor," she sang. And then after the rehearsal, when we Townies were alone, dissecting the Show in our adults cabal, Frances announced that she didn't appreciate my hang-ups, and she told us all, all of us with balls - me, Gary (and her wild child, Danny) - that she was fed up with the leaching of her energies,

an activity, this, sucking, which "all you men and boys do."
Hence, she explained, the rage behind the Kitchen Floor Stomp.

"Well, we weren't going to have any secrets," I said.

"And now we don't. Fuck you too."

"Take it like a man," I said.

"So now we've cleared the air," said Gary.

"Okay, Pasha," said Frances. I was Pasha in those days,
though Frances was not yet Vie. "So what do you want to do?"
asked Frances.

I shrugged.

"What do you want to do in the show? What do you want to
show us?"

"I don't know. I guess I'd just like to strut."

"So strut," said Frances. "Get up there and show us your
stuff. Strut!" But I was shy and tongue-tied by such an
unfriendly challenge. I went home in a huff and wrote "A Strut
for Alice".

A Strut for Alice

I'm a tower of passion
and a cauldron of wisdom and truth
I've been perceived as a power quite smashing
'cause I'm so perfectly balanced hard and smooth
and nobody fucks with Pasha
but that ain't because I'm uncouth
I ain't tread on your tail yet
sister don't hedge your bet
take a seat with your brothers
you ain't deified yet

Alice remember the Queen of Hearts
she was raving right through from the start
I know the tarts that she baked
were really hot cakes
but the knave who enjoyed those tarts
remember the liberties he gave you

me babe I just wanna be another sort of caterpillar
remembering what the dormouse said
feed your head Flower
or you ain't never gonna see no butterflies

I read Kano my poem. Kano lived up stairs from me in our not-quite-a-commune on College Terrace. "It's a song," said Kano and he gave me two chords and a melody. "A Strut for Alice" became my musical offering in the revue. The Body Show, our sophomore revue, was turning into a musical. We did "The Kitchen Floor Stomp" and "A Strut for Alice" and half a dozen other songs, mostly Frances's compositions, Frances and Richard's. Richard was one of the students, one of the twins' boy friends. He was our guitarist and he helped Frances with the melodies. Gary played drums and Kano played bass. We took the Body Show to Edinburgh and performed it as a fringe event at the Festival in 1975. The Scotsman deigned to reviewed us. "More painful than a visit to the dentist," they said.

"Do you remember him sitting there all tight arsed," said Frances. "Too frigging full of himself to see this is a work in progress."

"Something's going on and you don't know what it is, do you Mr. Jones?" sang Gary.

After the Body Show Frances, Gary and Richard stayed together as a band. They went punk and became "Poison Girls". Meanwhile the Brighton Council approved the proposal for a Community Centre. There would be salaries. An old warehouse in the Upper Lanes was leased. Frances was asked to direct the Centre. She contemplated this for several weeks, but Poison Girls had caught her. She was forty years old. Life would pass her if she just blinked her eye. She was a Punk Rocker now. She became Vie Subversa. The Poisons rehearsed at the Community Centre for a spell. And Frances and Richard became lovers. Gary stayed with the band, as the drummer, and with the extended family. He explained that he had invested too much in the children (Frances's children) to quit. The Poison evolved into a way of life. The extended family moved up to London and beyond to the Essex suburbs with its cheaper rent, larger house, next door to another band, more Punkers, and next to the Common. No other houses around to be disturbed.

The band enjoyed a little recognition among the Punk cognizanti. Ten years later, 1985, I was living in Toronto, studying Alternative Medicine. The Poisons did a small North American tour. Well, they played Philadelphia (where one of the Body Show twins was living) and Newark, and Toronto. They had a following in Newark and in Toronto. About four hundred fans turned up at Lee's Palace. "Frances, you're God!" the Punk beside me shouted.

I spent the next day with the Poisons. They spoke of Frances's fiftieth birthday bash. They hired Brixton Hall and all the Punk bands came and played a Poison Girls songs in tribute, bands including luminaries like the Buzzcocks and the Boomtown Rats. Neil made a giant crow (a Poisons' image that) that flew down a wire, wings flapping, from the gallery to the stage.

Neil was one of those unassuming persons who make it their function to be of service. When I met Frances and Gary, Neil was often round Sudeley Street just helping out. And soon after we met, Neil started looking after me too. Little things and bigger things. Things I couldn't do for myself, and things I could but that Neil choose to do for me. Why do I mention Neil. I am embarrassed and ashamed that after I left to return to America in search of a trade and profession I lost touch with Neil. I didn't extend him the courtesy of my continued attention and gratitude, and I think he may have liked that, some recognition. I could have returned the favour. I think that he, like most of us, enjoyed approval, and I don't think I ever adequately showed it.

Neil. There are the loud and the quiet, and the sometimes loud, like me. Neil was quiet where Pasha wanted to strut and

Vie was as big as the sky. It is not a gender thing, though, the fore-stage, backstage continuum. Just another parameter.

Gary was a quiet one too, though he pushed himself forward in an effort to be of service: he played the drums in a rock and roll punk band, for God's sake. He spoke of how it felt to meet with young punkers at their gigs, Poison Girl's gigs, to meet with skinheads, punk fans, in the washrooms and discuss with them their thought and feeling towards skinhead Nazism and/or anarchism and this was real politics, nitty-gritty stuff: not like his academically inspired social agitation of the sixties. "The Sussex paint throwing incident was one of my class projects," he told me.

"Oh," said I. "I thought it was Sean Linehan and that American dude." [1]

"Yes," said Gary, "but who supplied the paint and the idea?" I[2] raised my eyebrows. "It was a class project," said Gary. "I wanted to give my London Polytechnic kids an example of impact in social engagement."

Once upon a time in nineteen sixty eight when we thought the times were changing, the American Press Attaché [3] came down to Sussex University to explain why America was waging war in Indochina and somebody[4] threw red paint over him - which we felt was a pretty legitimate thing to do, a relatively nonviolent response to the war. A few days later the University suspended[5] Sean and the American grad. An urgent meeting of the student body was
convened where it was pointed out that Sean had had no trial or hearing. He could not defend himself. And who were his accusers? What evidence was there of his involvement? The student union wanted to know, or at least the left and the hippies[6] wanted to know. A spokesperson for the right wing students[7] got up to defend the University's actions "We've got photographs!" he said waving a manila envelope.

"Fair cop," thought the student body, and it shrugged. On to other business. But then someone grabbed the envelope and peeked at the picture. "Hey, these don't show anything. Just somebody's back." [8]

The mood of the assembly pendalummed. Even would-be docile students don't like being duped. A strike was instantly put to the vote and passed.. Sean must be given a chance to defend himself. Justice must be seen to be done. No classes for Sean, no classes for anyone!

The strike had the active support of a large caucus of enthusiasts and the grudging respect of the bulk of the student body. Few tried to cross the picket lines.

Asa Briggs, a noted liberal[9] historian and the Vice Chancellor of the University, offered to meet with the students to discuss our grievances. The administration in those days was housed in a single story red brick building near the rear of the campus. They were all red brick, the buildings at Sussex, which was the architectural theme of the campus, red brick among trees and lawns and sidewalks on which we stood surrounding the administration building with signs and megaphones, dozens, even hundreds of us. "No Sean, no classes! No Sean, no classes!" Briggs came out to speak to us in a rationale, non-confrontational manner and we listened respectfully. He spoke about the Universities sociopolitical situation; we were supported by the Government through grants, and we were not above the law. The student body had invited the Press Attaché and so the University owed him some respect and protection. The administration had irrefutable evidence of Sean's involvement, Briggs claimed. [10] Further, Sean's suspension would only be till the end of the fall term, another few weeks. His grades need not suffer[11], and he could return in the new years, in January, and he could sit his exams then[12]. "We all need to be reasonable," said Briggs. With the word "reasonable" the picketing students let out a groan which still echoes in my mind these decades on. "Reasonable?" Good grief. Reasonably they send us to slaughter. Reasonably they poison our air and water.[13]

A few years on I met Sean on a bus. He was a graduate with honours in "Sociology"[14] and he was, for a spell[15], a bus conductor. "Its the end of my shift," he said. "Can you come for a beer."

"Will I keep my honorary Irish status if I refuse," I asked.

"You will not."

So over Guinness we discussed the state of Ireland, the world and the Sussex Student Strike. "You know the scary thing," said Sean, "was that I only told six people, all good friends, and one of them probably ratted me out."

"And I was one of the six."

"Ah, but your an honorary Irishman," said Sean with a wink.

"Tank God," I says.

So what's this all about? It's the loose ends of my Brighton stories, Frances and Gary and the Student's Strike, and the theme, if there is one, is our need to be heard, and we are heard through our passion as much as through our reason. So raise your glass, and here's to Ireland, and sing us a song.

"I'm a tower of passion…" [16]

Sean has recently (27 July 2005) sent comments. Thanks to the internet they are appended here as endnotes. These are Sean Linehan's comments:

1. that American dude - Mike Klein
2. the idea was to throw pig's blood, but the abattoir was closed, so Jill Parker suggested paint
3. Mr. Beers
4. it was Sean L
5. technically 'rusticated' which came from the Oxbridge of yore when naughty students were sent back to their country estates for a while - Mike and I were not allowed to go on campus or even Falmer Park which was a public park owned by Brighton Council!. It was my last term before Final Exams and I lost my grant and was not even entitled to unemployment benefit because I was technically still a student even with no income. I worked night shift at Sunblest Bakeries to help my then wife (Sandra) and I to survive. I also had a severe breakdown because of the work and stress and pressure and drinking and drugging and some adultery my wife found out about [it was the 60s after all]. I was committed to a psychiatric hospital after a near fatal suicide attempt [whilst there I tried twice more and failed again and again]. I was ambulanced into the University Medical centre heavily sedated. Once there I was given speed to 'wake me up' and sit the Finals papers. If I got too manic I was sedated again. If I got too sleepy, I was given another pill. How I managed to pass the exams I'll never know because it was done in a blur of upping and downing and confusion.
6. I became a teacher of English! - habits die hard!
7. Chris Irwin – grrrrr
8. It was my back, but of an entirely different incident where we tried to get into the Senior Common Room earlier to harangue the Attaché
9. I called the meeting where I was rusticated, a 'Star Chamber', and he was suitably abashed.
10. we all asked to see this evidence and to know the names of the accusers which is the basic right of everyone under the law - but the University is 'not above the law' – hmmmmm
11. ....er yes, and how could that be when Mike and I were not allowed to meet tutors, attend lectures, use the Library or communicate with the University in any way
12 ? (*I've misplaced footnote #12 Oops. I think it detailed some hardship around sitting his exams, or not being able to sit them on time*)
13. reasonably the good historian Asa told us that we could not judge the war in Vietnam until we had 'historical perspective - We had evidence then that the war was dangerously escalating; that civilians were being targeted deliberately; that the US was planning to bomb in Chinese territory and that 'tactical' nuclear weapons might be employed. The fact that some of these

did not come about was precisely because of negative 'domestic and foreign reactions'. We were actually helping to stop the escalation into China and the use of nuclear devices by our actions. If we had believed Asa and all the Namby Pambies, the history they would have studied with perspective would have been much worse!

14. actually, ironically, American Studies

15. a year

16. Well, Norman, I hope I've added historical perspective to your reflections. They were heady days and despite everything that happened to me, I still feel immensely proud to have thrown paint over that man. Bertrand Russell sent a magic telegram to Asa in which he said, "I heartily endorse the actions of these honourable students. I will buy that miserable man a new suit if the Americans will agree to get out of Viet Nam."

I worked my year on Brighton buses which restored my sanity because I had been a Manchester bus conductor before going to Sussex. They liked to add the yeast of working class 'rough' to the fine wheat of middle class trendies in those days.

(... Sean filled in a brief history of himself since those days (which I have seriously abridged). He worked as a teacher and ...) founded and ran an organisation called 'Wage Peace'.

... I became an education officer dealing with work-experience for schools and colleges in Islington and Camden for 3 years. I then became an Advisory Teacher for Disaffected Students in Southwark and established anti-bullying policies and tried to get non-attenders back into school.

I then went around the world backpacking for a year going through the States to Fiji and New Zealand and all around Australia. I then went to Thailand, Cambodia and Vietnam (where I cried to see the tribute they made in the War Museum to those of us who supported their struggle). ...

... I went to Northern Ireland where I taught in Belfast, Crumlin and Lisburn for a few years. Last year I taught in an EBD (Educational and Behavioural Difficulties) School in East Belfast. It was not easy to deal with the worst behaved kids in Northern Ireland (all Protestant and in para-military groups) being an English [*I always thought Sean was Irish - and that he had made me an honouary Irishman!*] Catholic (albeit non-believing that bullshit)

... When I get back to NI, I shall be teaching kids who cannot go to school because of illness or badness in their own homes.

Regards,

Sean

A MAN OF GOD

Philip tells a story about the Swami Vinoba Bhavi. Philip spent three months at the guru's ashram in Puna. The guru was a teacher of some renown. The day Philip arrived at the ashram it was swarming with police and military. The Prime Minister of India, Indira Ghandi, was visiting the ashram to consult with and seek advice from Vinoba. Then she was whisked away in a helicopter and slowly the troops and police dispersed.

The next morning, when Philip came out into the courtyard, he saw an old man in a loin cloth sweeping the yard. Here was the great Vinoba Bhavi. A small wizened man, he stood not much more than five foot tall. Thin arms, thin chest. A calm and grace suffused him focused as he was on his task.

A disciple, a "nun" in saffron robe, approached him. "Babaji," she said. "Why are you sweeping? A great man like you, all the world comes to you for your advice. Why not leave such a menial task to others?"

Swami Vinoba bent over and reached to the ground. He picked up a small pebble. "Ram," he said (Ram being one of the names of God). Then lovingly laid the pebble back down where he had found it and picked up a small tangle of thread, lint, and fluff. "God,' he said, and put it down again. He picked up a small dried leaf…

THE LADY WITH THE BOOTS.

The lady with the boots should be a private story. Carolyn was an enigma, even to herself.

We met, we touched, but we danced to different bands, and I was entranced. She, though, was lost in the confusion of her body, and that's the story, and that's private, but I'm going to kiss and tell.

I met Carolyn in the Brighton's Lanes, the Upper Lanes, near the market. Rob and I were talking about his "Art Night" when Carolyn entered the shop. My jaw dropped. Her knee-high boots accented her long legs and she became for me forever "the lady with the boots".

The shop where we met had art and object d'art, some tasteful secondhand cloths, and tables - a coffee shop. Small, yet somehow spacious. Rob and I had been speaking of his "Art Space Evening". He planned to hold this event in the crypt above Rached's café down by the Arcades. Down at the beach Rached, Birghton's Sufi guru, sold sausage and chips in his fast café to the hordes from London. Fries Fries Fries in the bustle of the weekend. These arcades, fronting on the beach, had crypt-like rooms above them (under the sidewalk, the "boardwalk") and here Rob planned to hold his Art Space event. We would drum and jam, recite and perform in the quietus, the fall and failure of the "Counter Culture". This was the mid-nineteen seventies and I was quite lost in my life… but I got up and went over to try and charm the lady with the boots and I invited her to Rob's Performance, his "be in" Space.

The lady with the boots did drop by at Rob's art thing, but very late, when we were closing up. "I had another appointment and was held up," she said.

I saw her in the town after that, pushing David Spender round. David was a crip. A CP spastic. Couldn't speak, but Carolyn could read where he spastically pointed his nose. David was doing a masters degree in Social Science, or Chemical

Engineering, or Hawkin's Physics, and the lady with the boots was typing his thesis and his nurse maid, or maybe just nurse maid. Maybe he had other means of writing.

The lady with the boots was chaste with me, for the most part. Eventually she went off to Australia. Meanwhile, I courted her. We became friends. For a while we were quite close. She told me about her sexuality. She could only really "get off" in slightly S and M contexts - could only climax with spanking (she had friends in London), or, or, actually other bizarre or perverse situations (fucking in a boyfriends sports car, her ass in the gearshift knob, then, too, she'd climaxed, or once or twice when she'd let David spastically lick her bosom), and she thought she might be a bit of psych case. Sexually at least, though she wasn't unduly alarmed, nor did she find being a nursemaid in any way demeaning. She came from that part of Provincial England (the upper lower middle class) where such a position was quietly quite professional.

I met her parents once. We drove to visit them in Bedfordshire. They ran a guest house… a small hotel. A quaint white building on a fork in a minor road on the edge of a minor village.

The lady with the boot was rather tall, slim, athletic. Ponies and polo. A perfect lady and a natural blond. She was a lovely, kind person. A little defensive: shy almost, or reserved, reticent. I was drawn. She was most definitely a sexual challenge. She told me that the reason she had been late at our first date, Rob's Art thing, was that she'd visited some young man who offered a massage and she got laid (though not ignited).

She came down to Wales with me for a few days to visit my kids, taking them off with us to stay at the Carmarthan Farm and sleeping upstairs - this our second night together: we had spent a chaste night the night before in someone country cottage - sleeping upstairs at the Carmarthan Farm, with the kids softly tucked in a tumble of mattresses and eiderdowns, sleeping bags, dark room beneath the eaves above the house and cuddled up to her I made love to the lady with the boots whom I had so admired (she who took my breath away). And that was it. Though we were friends, we never gelled.

A while later she went to visit Marrakech. I don't remember the circumstances, but I suggested she look you up, Serge, for you are the gate to Marrakech; its finest host.

I also sent a message to a Hassan. Hassan was an honest merchant, a young man who, with his younger brother, Mohammed, ran a "souk", a store that sold kaftans and jellabas and rugs and drums and brass and silver - Moroccan ware. Hassan and Mohammed's shop was the first you'd come upon walking from the main square - the Ja Mal Fna - to the Casbah, the "Medina", and when I'd been there, in Morocco, a year or two before, I had spent time in their souk. Smoked kif and drank mint tea with Hassan and with Mohammed, his brother - Mohammed, with his curly afro and bright eyes, cool kif kid in kaftan - a smart quick mother with an ego as bushy as his hair - "I am a friend of Cat Stevens. When he's in town he hangs out with me," said Mohammed.

I had brought trinkets: Mylar "prism" (diffraction grating). Rainbow prismatic Mylar was treasure in those days - rare and mind blowing. I brought these trinkets as offerings and Mohammed bagged my last. Hassan, quiet and sincere, but not good looking, had commented how Mohammed bagged everything. I told Hassan I'd send him one, and I did, with a note. It said, "Hassan, Mohammed bags all the stuff, but you've got all the heart," and I sent a Mylar (rainbow) sheriff's star to Marrakech for Hassan with the lady with the boots.

Meanwhile, Serge, she met you and you fell in love, totally infatuated, bewitched by this English rose. The lady with the boots, so beautiful at the villa in Agadir where you drove for the day and an evening. So demure and chaste and fascinating. I witnessed the depth of your adoration in the besotted letter you sent to our friend, Tee, which she translated for me from your poetic French. And the lady with the boots spoke to me also, telling me how wonderful you were and how in love with her, and how chaste she was with you. Meanwhile she delivered my message - "Hassan, Mohammed bags all the stuff..."

"Ah," said sun-faced Mohammed. "This is for me," and pocketed my gift to Hassan's, and bagged her too, the lady with the boots; fucked her bum, most evenings. After she'd leave you, she'd go round to his place, to his rude embrace.

Poor Hassan too. No trinket, and no word from the stranger.

And what happened to the lady with the boots? In the house she had moved into in Brighton there was a pleasant postgraduate student, Kevin, awake and attractive, and just a friend, and eventually, oh, after a couple of years, they went off to Australia together. I believe they married. A happy ending, I think. He seemed the happiest, most straight forward and natural of fellows.

For me, though, the story ends with a realisation many years later. Through those years I had thought this story was a testament to my quality as a lover, for she had told me that when we'd made love softly in Wales, she had come... "What a rooster I was," I crowed to myself. But later, recently, I realised that it was probably rather that that attic in Wales, with the children quietly sleeping over there further under the eaves... that balling there with the children asleep in the room may have felt perverse to her (though to me we felt so gentle together).

So here is the story for Serge, who doesn't speak English, who just speaks French, to tell you in a language you cannot read of ports and harbours and ships that pass. A braggart's story.

And what is the point of this story? You tell me. For me it is just a story: a kiss and tell.

ICARUS

I was telling Gerri about my burnt out poet friend. How he was the brightest kid at school and went up to Oxford to study law. He wrote poetry, and one of his poems became a Rock and Roll hit, briefly. He dropped out and fell apart, I learned bumping into him twenty years later. So what good are "brains", I wondered. His life is a toilet bowl.

Gerri said she understood. "Back in the sixties Rock and Roll had cornered the market on orgasm. You just can't imagine the power and glory. I had married a Rock and Roller. I was dancing on Olympus. One day you're you, you're me. The next day suddenly you are very special. Over night. You scribble on a napkin, everybody wants to know what it means. The luxury. You could do anything. Close the office for a week, hire a suite at the Ritz, drink Champaign. Call in the best dope. The party was eternal, for those on the inside."

"I was flying down to LA," she said, "with the baby in my belly. The candy man had insisted that I carry five joints of Nepalese down to my man. "They're special. No hassle." As Bobby Dylan said, you had to believe you could walk through walls. I slipped the joints into my cigarette case."

"On the plane I was sitting beside these two heads. One looked like Frank Zappa. The one beside me looked like one of the Grateful Dead. He asked me if I knew where he could score some gear, some smoke. I was an innocent and I had no idea. I said so."

"It turns out he was a narc and he was extraditing the Zappoid after some big dope bust."

"Well, some hours later I remembered the Nepalese and I tapped the Deadhead's shoulder and told him I'd just remembered I had five joints on me and he was welcome to them."

" "Oh, I only need two," he said." "
" "No. Take them all." "
" "No," he said. He took two." "

"You'd think the Zappoid might have said something to tip me off, but no."

"So we were disembarking, and the Deadhead just pressed right up against me on the ramp. I thought that was strange. And as soon as my feet touched the runway he reached round to splay ————————————————————— his badge in my face. And that was the end of my life. It all went sour after that. Oh, I got off with a warning, but the court case was interminable. Luckily my Drummer Man never turned up at the airport. I was praying he wouldn't walk in on this bummer. He didn't, and he walked right out of my life."

"I stayed with Mama Cass waiting for my court date. But the party was over. I'm a bank clerk now. And I'm bitter. It's not fun telling your daughter, "That's your father on the radio, in that movie up there on the screen," and you're living in a one bedroom walk-up and not enough money to buy her a bicycle."

"I think that's what happened to your poet too. He stayed too long at the party, and not long enough."

MIND BODY DIALOGUE IN A CLINICAL SETTING

As Sister Catherine pointed out to me once, apropos of body, mind and spirit, "It's not a third part mind, a third part body, a third part spirit. It's a hundred percent mind, a hundred percent body, a hundred percent spirit." She also noted that spirit is intrinsically mysterious. Then again, so is mind - many scientists feel they can reduce consciousness and experience to a pattern of electrical charge and that, to me, is pretty mysterious. And that leaves us the body. We've learnt lots about the body, and yet that too, in its aliveness, is still a mystery. We are doomed then, and blessed, to walk and work in mystery.

When I was studying Barral's Visceral Manipulation (with Frank Lowen), I was feeling the sigmoid colon, pulling on the tension in the sigmoid mesocolon of one of my class mate and there was this "knot", this tension in Lee's mesocolon that wouldn't release with breath or through simple intentional exercises (like asking, "How would this energy like to release?" and then inviting the patient to visualize that release). So we did a "scenario". "Scenario" work is what I call variants on going inside, taking whatever resources you need to feel safe, saying what you want to, doing what you want, and having it turn out the way you want; that is, moving the scenario towards resolution.

"Go inside. Into this spot..." I was tugging on Lee's abdomen, lower left quadrant, on this fascial locus of tension, contraction, that I identified and labeled as relating to the sigmoid mesocolon. "What do you see?"

"I see a door," Lee said. He visualizes easily.

"Can you open the door?"

Lee laughed, "Yes." (Nowadays I'd ask first, "Is it safe to open the door?")

Lee opened the door on to his childhood front yard, the path leading to the gate. Down by the gate was a German Sheppard that had bit him when he was twelve years old. "He gave me this scar," Lee said pointing to his brow.

"Go inside and say what you want to say, do what you want to do, and have it turn out how you wish it to."

Lee "went inside". He reported after that he told the dog to stay; the dog stayed. He told the dog to sit; the dog sat.

Meanwhile, I was "pulling" gently on the mesocolon, and at some point the tension just dissolved, like butter, and with this there was a little blast of heat!

Now, this underlines and/or suggests the following: that we store our traumas in the body, and in particular in the belly; that with trauma there may be a tightening in the gut, and we anchor events, and reactions, constellations of experience, in the viscera, first as a contraction of smooth muscle, a cramp or a spasm in the mesentery or mesocolon, for example, and that as that knot or tension is held, the collagen changes its conformation, coils, shortens; and then that contracture holds a memory, as it were, or rather it is a key to an "association", to a constellation, a pattern of event and issues. So, we have here a mechanism for repression: store it in the belly and ignore it.

Why in the belly? Well, the feeling in the guts is part of the experience and… we can make these anchors, these contractures there and… the belly is a convenient place to ignore, and hence repress. Perhaps we simply use this mechanism because it's available. Like so much else, it may be fortuitous.

The amazing thing, to me, in the incident I described, was that the collagen would release like that, in an instant, as Lee revisited and re-wrote his drama. The collagen unwound releasing the energy, the heat, that that change of conformation, that that coiling had held these years. Our collagen, our fascia, is alive. It is responsive.

One might ask, is this the only mechanism, or the main mechanism for repression? It is part of the picture.

Accompanying a trauma the muscles in the gut contract, the collagen conforms, contracts, and takes up a contracted posture, position. And if you multiply these contractions you can get contractures of surgical proportions.

Cynthia had a contracture in her gut, in the later third of her ileum, five centimeters long on the barium swallow. She had not eaten, or passed stool, for eight days and was scheduled for surgery. I was asked to visited her in hospital on the eve of her operation. We talked, some about white flowers, her mother and white funereal flowers. We also did some CranioSacral hands-on "unwinding" over and under that contractured spot in her gut along with "visualizing". Cyn saw a prawn-like pink embryo, in her gut.

Did it have a name? I asked.

"Maybe Cynthia." (The patient's name was not Cynthia.)

Did Maybe Cynthia have a message?

"Yes. The message is "No"."

"No?"

"No, I don't have to die." And with this ideation, realization, there was a "release" and my hands seemed to move three inches laterally (back towards me) and, after a pause, a second "release". My hands followed the tissue and now they seemed to travel three inches superior (cephalad). And Cynthia and I "knew" that the problem had resolved, that the contracture had released.

She was radiant.

In the morning Cynthia passed stool and she was hungry, so instead of surgery, she had breakfast. The hospital served her bacon and eggs!

Ah! the "three inch" movement of my hands that appeared to accompany the "unwinding", the release of the constriction? It had to be in some sense symbolic - a ritual that I had unconsciously devised - or at the very least it was a gross amplification. And the vectors, the direction was "wrong". The release, very likely, was radial, of sphincter like muscles, not lateral.

And that brings to mind another unworldly aspect of this sort of bodywork, this dialoguing. In the Barral's visceral work, to work with the kidneys we lay our palms, our hypothenars, on the abdominal wall at the level of the bottom pole of the "kidneys" and we follow the movement. But the kidneys are three or more inches away (at the back of the abdomen)! So I often say to the patient that the contact is like a Star Trek tractor beam. Similarly we can "stretch" the ureters by placing a thumb down near the pubis to pin down the bottom of the ureter, down near the bladder, while placing the other hand on the inferior pole of the kidney, as described above, and pushing it, encouraging the kidney in a cephalad, a head-ward, direction to stretch the ureter. And patients will usually report that they can feel the stretching of the ureter, though it's physically far from our contact on the anterior wall of the abdomen. More tractor beams, but it leaves us with the question as to whether this manipulation of the abdomen is mechanical, "energetic", or symbolic? And, of course, the answer is probably all of these.

John Upledger, of CranioSacral Therapy, believes that we store our "repressions" in the viscera because of a relative stability there, and the striate muscles of the musculoskeletal system, the muscles of movement (and their fascia) move about too much to act as storehouses. Yet there certainly can be restriction in the locomotary fascia and these, like the tension in the visci, can be released through intention "energetically". They will interact (as determinants and products) with posture and attitude.

Upledger sees symptoms as a way that we get the body to talk to the self: - vehicles of Freud's return of the repressed. Sometimes we can see them as metaphors. (Michael Vertolli, my herb teacher, says symptoms are simply the body's best way of dealing with a problem. Suppress a symptoms and the body will find the next best way.)

Another tangent: there's a "clever" thought I had about the gut long ago when I was young which I've never written down anywhere, and it's almost relevant here. As a child, and infant, like many I suffered on occasion quite nasty "stomach" pains, cramps. And from the age of twelve I was in therapy. I was raised a "Freudian". The thought was this: that the gut is experienced more as a sequence of events in time than as a spatial structure. The gut's rather randomly there inside in our somewhat amorphous bellies. So, I thought, what the intestines represent is sequence and consequence and that it is the archetypal snake, serpent, and dragon.

We should talk, at least briefly, about safety, and about projection, and boundaries, and "copping out".

Safety: remember to ask the patient about safety whenever you suspect it might be an issue. Of course, resistance grows as we approach the repressed. One way of dealing with this is to dialogue with the higher self. In CranioSacral work, Upledger often get his patients to initiate such a dialogue. Dialogue with "higher self", be that spirit of intuition or whatever, can be employed to help look after safety, and indeed, to help with almost anything.

Projection: when we leave the therapy to the patient we can minimize our projections, but when we contribute there is always a risk. I try to stay aware of how prone I am to project and I often preface my contributions with a caveat warning about projection.

But, how much should the facilitator contribute? When I was studying "dialoguing and imaging" at the Upledger Institute, there was one T.A. who pulled virtually all her patients off the table to try and rebirth them. She tried to make everyone conform to her conception.

How can we make sure we stay with the patient's agenda if we contribute? And should we contribute?

Marsha came to my office for chiropractic for low back pain, which we helped, but she liked the CranioSacral work and she returned for more. So I was sitting with my hands over and under her right thigh when a thought arrived which I felt called to voice. (I've never said anything like this before or since.) I said, "It's as though there's a microfilm embedded in your thigh."

"Oh my God!" said Marsha. "I dreamed last night I was in a submarine. I was a spy and they were looking for the microfilm. It was hidden in my left thigh. They tied me to the periscope."

Marsha had forgotten her dream after waking and during the day, but she had never repressed what it alluded to. She told me that from the age of three till she was five her mother used to take her down into the basement, tie her up to a round pillar, a cylindrical floor support, and whip her thighs with electrical wire. From the age of three Marsha knew that her mother was mad, crazy. She was still looking after her mother, at twenty-five, but about leave home to travel east. She sent me a happy postcard from Katmandu. She had never forgotten the abuse, but she had never spoken of it (so spirit engineered a dream, and something like telepathy, so that she would speak of it).

Mind, body, spirit overlap and the boundaries between them are not really understood. Contemplating the question I get tongue tied and boggled.

And "boundaries"? I'm left with the New Ager's dedication to the "highest good".

We might also have segued from "projection", to how often we may be "missing the point" and from this to the danger of "copping out". My friend Vanessa practiced a variety of mind body dialogue out in B.C. She had a male patient with a pelvic cancer. He visualized the tumor as having five tentacles. After surgery the tentacles were still there. Vanessa and he dealt with three of them - they disappeared from Frank's image - but then they got into a bind. Frank had abused his teenage stepdaughter. Vanessa and he felt that one of the remaining tentacles related to this, however, when they came to address this issue, the patient started acting out very "suggestively" in a manner

Vanessa found she did not want to handle. The eminent innovator of the therapy Vanessa practiced was about to lead a large seminar in Toronto. Vanessa raised donations in her clinic to fly her patient to Toronto so the Eminent could work with him. The Eminent choose to work with him in public session where the cancer "told" the patient that the issue, at issue, was around his creativity: that what he needed to do was to give up his hack day-job, editing, and work on his novel. Vanessa felt strongly that this was a huge cop out. She felt let down.

How do we guard against copping out? Ah. We can return to the feel in the body. Phil Walsh, in his scenario work, which he calls Autosomatic Training, uses feeling - feeling are usually located in the body - and we can use feeling as a guide towards truth and towards completeness.

I feel I should tell you about Gorginski's mice: Greg Gorginski was a colleague of David Ader, the author of psychoneuro-immunology. They were working with tumor-prone mice and wondering why tumors manifested in some mice and not others. Using an "Open Field Test" they found that the tumors manifested in the "emotional" mice (the scored of micturation and defecation in the first five minutes of a stressful experience, the open field, and, in all probability, a measure of autonomic sympathetic tone). So Greg bred the most "emotional" and the least "emotional" mice, for eight generations, till he had some very emotional and some very calm mice indeed. Then in the ninth generation he cross-foster the mice: he gave the "emotional" pups to calm mothers to raise, to suckle and the calm pups to "emotional" mothers: and it's who gives you suck that determines your emotional tone!

Now I assume it's the "vibe" of your mother that sets your tone, but I was telling this story to an eminent doctor, a pain specialist, and she assumed it would be some factor in the milk. And indeed we might expect more adrenaline and adrenaline derivatives in the "emotional" milk. So is this body or mind, and where are the boundaries? The dialogues between us are usually of both mind (verbal) and body-talk... and what else?

Finally, I'd like to tell you about Michael's liver flukes. After returning from the south Michael was determined that he had parasites (though stool sample were negative). In my office Michael visualized and dialogued with his flukes. They saw his liver as a golden sun. There were dark patched in his liver. The liver flukes ate and cleaned up the dark parts. They worship his liver and tended it, and if Michael would give up junk food and coffee they would agree to pass on (through their eggs, their progeny) to another host.

Sometimes our symptoms are more concerned about our well being then we are, even parasites from a distant phyla, and even if it is all just in our minds. Sometimes our symptoms are metaphors, though looking too hard for metaphor can sometimes be another cop out. Sometimes our dialogue may be completely off point: stuff and nonsense.

Mind, body, spirit, where is the divide? I had another clever thought the other day, though probably one that's as old as the hills: -

There is more to the mind than the body. Though the mind embraces the body, the body is only a small part of the mind. And one can say the same of spirit and mind: spirit embraces the mind, but mind is only a small part of spirit. So we walk and work in the mysterious.

(There is a more complete discussion of Cynthia's story in *Norman Allan: the story for Ezra: Book Two, Secrets, Chapter On, Maybe Cynthia*, posted at www.normanallan.com.)

A MEETING WITH
MARIAN WOODMAN

In October 2006 Jill Lazenby suggested I submit a paper for the
conference she was working on, on Mind Body Dialogue, a
conference at Toronto University's OISE given in honour of
Marian Woodman, who would be the principle speaker and
receive a "lifetime achievement award". The conference would
be held in June 2007.

Oh wow! Have I got some things to say about "dialoguing"?

I spent November writing and rewriting - I usually need to
tweak and tweak for weeks and weeks - and by December I had
a paper I was proud of. And it was accepted! The paper was
little long. It's most of what I know about "dialoguing with the
body" in 10 pages, but if I really motored I could deliver it in 20
minutes. Twenty years in twenty minutes.

As the conference approached I looked at the schedule on-line.
Ooh oh. Apart form the keynote speakers, all the other papers
would be delivered in divided up "paper sessions", eight at a
time, in separate rooms. I had had visions of standing on a
podium lecturing a full hall. Never mind. I was going to make
the best of this.

This reminded me of a "trade show" a year before when I
hadn't "make the best…".

My friend John worked as the "Wellness Coordinator" for a
very large concern just down the street from my office. John,
from the time he met me, spoke about organizing a little
wellness trade show (for me?) at his institution. He took him a
year, and when it happened it was a triumph, for the most part.
He had about 18 exhibitors in a small hall in the cooperation's
home office. He put aside a special place for me at the back of
the hall so that I could consult and treat. And then he arranged
tables in front of me in a separate row so that nobody could get

to me. I suggested the row needed some rearranging, but that didn't happen. Perhaps a third of the people who came into the hall walked past my table. Two thirds never even saw me. No biggie, maybe, but I didn't grin from ear to ear. I made due.

At the end of the conference I congratulated John, I thought, very warmly, for his event, all in all, was a great success.

I didn't speak to John for a few weeks and when I did he told he that I was the only one to complain at the event and the only person who did not phone him, as a follow up, to thank him. Up until this time John and I used to lunch together every other week, and I visited his country haunt not infrequently. After this, though, we've met twice in the year and only on my initiation. Ho hum. "So it goes."

So at the mind body conference I was not going to repeat these mistakes. I was going to make the best of it. I was going to be a real "half full glass" guy.

Now, my story, my paper is awesome, I think. Take a look, I say laughing. So it was a quite a let down to find I wasn't going to deliver it to a throng. And then the first keynote speaker talked in circles about very little. And the first paper session, tiny audiences and in the session I chose, one guy talking about a project on "talking circles" in the native tradition and he did a study, focus groups. He got to talk to three, three! people, and generalize from that. (Stop being so negative, Norman. It was a good intent. Nice people. The second paper was a study with just as small a population, unfinished work, and empty... but I listened, I listened , I was present. And I talked to people. And I had a good time, virtue being it's own reward and all.)

That first day, Monday, the conference started late - the subway wasn't running for a while in the morning - so after another, for me, empty plenum session paper (the professor sang and played guitar! with modest talent), I missed the workshop session (divided again, eight to choose from) to go home walk and feed the dogs before going to try and catch Marion Woodman's address to the conference that evening in the auditorium. But, it was my birthday and I had another engagement, so I couldn't stay long.

First a head of a department delivered a eulogy and biography - fascinating, yes, but a flat delivery and thirty five minutes.

Marion Woodman, at 45, decided to go to Zurich to study to become a Jungian analyst. She went on to become an icon to the new age with her work on the unconscious and, particularly, her work on the feminine. I've not (yet) read Woodman, and I'd not yet seen her ever, but knew of her and her work. If someone says "Joseph Campbell" (the grandmaster of myth), I'd probably think, "and Marion Woodman". She was a luminary figure in certain sections of the counter-culture. But before she got to the stage there was a presenter to present the lifetime achievement award - another five minutes, and my time was running out, but I was cool. Making the best.

Marion Woodman is 81. Dignified, but no hard edges. It's all these privilege words that come to me: aristocratic, noble. Marion started by thanking the presenters, and, two minutes in, it was time for me to leave. Still I felt filled just to see this presence!

Tuesday I arrived early, again, to make the most... Through the long window I saw Marion Woodman arriving. I went to the foyer. Found her free. Offered her a copy of my poetry chapbook, "Incarnations". A pleasant, but not significant, meeting.

That morning Ms. Woodman was to lead a plenum workshop. Move the chairs, she said. Lie on the floor. Find a dream image.

Now, I couldn't find a decent recent dream image, but a childhood nightmare came to mind. A ten, an impressive dream about a great hole, and I'm on a ledge inside it, to deep to escape... and then I drifted off. (I'll have to ask Jill about the workshop!)

So to my paper delivery. An audience of six! And it didn't take 22 minutes. It only took 18. I could have gone slower. Oh.

Anticlimax. But I have the paper to post on my website where who, where who will read it?

My co-deliverer in this session had some interesting things to say about consciousness from Yogic-psychology perspective. I'll blog it later.

And in a little workshop in the afternoon it was pointed out that, in speech, it is vowel that carry most of the emotion.

So I learned stuff, a bit. And I met people, a few. And it was a good conference. But now it was over. My incisive paper unheard, virtually. I'd read to half a dozen pairs of ears and the wind, but I was making a much better go of it. I was making the best.

So finally I'm in the foyer - time to go home - and I think I'll just take one last look in the library where all the plenum session were.

Marion Woodman was sitting in an armchair, in the library, talking to a middle-aged follower or protégé, who was gushing and saying good-bye. Two younger enthusiasts, whom I knew from the conference, warm people, sat near. Their was space on the sofa opposite Marion, so I sat. The leave-taker finished and left and Ms. Woodman turned to me. "You wanted to talk to me?"

"Well yes, but I have no context," I said.

She beckoned me over. "So what brings you here," she asked.

I told her of my friend's invitation and my paper on mind body dialogue. "That's an important subject," said Marion. "Do you have a spare copy."

Yes! Instant karma for my (relatively) good attitude. I had to glow. What better audience could I ask for?

We talked for five, ten minutes. Mostly I talked, trying to elaborate very briefly on my thought that spirit is actively suppressing "scientific investigation" into the fringes of science and the paranormal (I will write of this at more length). And then Marion Woodman said to me, with just a little pomp (perhaps she introduced it with, "I've something to tell you").

"In any meeting," she said, "the most powerful presence there is the unconscious."

In any meeting, the most powerful presence there is the unconscious.

"Yes," I said, having my own little flash of insight, "because it connects to spirit."

And I had another insight. The snippet of a dream, the big trench, the big hole, it was "the unconscious".

(I was telling this story to my therapist, Phil Walsh, about being stuck on the ledge in this pit above the unconscious, Phil says he would advise me to just jump in. "Into all that shit and fire?" I demurred.

"You can flick off the shit," said Phil, "and fire purifies.")

So that's the story of my meeting with Marion Woodman. What a blessing. Thank you.

MY MULTIPLE FRIEND

I don't know how it ends, but Justin's story was beyond sensational, though I think he is sinking and by now he has probably sunk. I met Jus after he phoned to see if I could fix his rib. Coming into the office he announced, "You don't have to worry. We had a conference, twenty six of the leading personalities, we held a conference in the waiting room just now and we've agreed not to harm you." You know, I never had any fear with Jus, though he was six foot four and a body builder when we met, and some of his "alters" were as rough as tumble. Perhaps foolishly, I felt safe.

Jus had "put out" a rib working out at the gym. It was new for him to want to fix it, to want to avoid pain, to heal, but he had decided that he wanted to heal all the pains, and boy, was that a task. He had started taking therapy with the head of psychiatry at McPherson University Hospital. "We've discovered one hundred and five alternative personalities, so far, by hypnosis, Dr. Mann and I. I have more alters than any other Multiple on record."

Healing, pains - Jus told me he had spent his summers fishing on the high seas. One summer he broke his thigh bone a few inches above the knee. "Snapped it clean through. I walked around on it for six months. The doctors couldn't believe it," but Jus had spent that half year in the personalities of several alters that felt no pain.

The year Jus came to see me I ended up with five patients with Multiple Personality Disorder, five MPDs, in my practice. It started with Marla, who came for a low back problem and stayed for some CranioSacral relaxation/ counseling. She was a "multiple", but not, on the surface, dramatic. (Her alters were lots and lots of frightened infants that stayed hidden in public. Marla felt comfortable with me, and she sent Jus, who she knew from a self-help network. Then Jus sent two friends, acquaintances. And there was another, a fifth MPD, I discovered in my practice, or maybe I "generated" that one...)

I started reading about Multiple Personality Disorder. It's a survival technique when the mind is just overwhelmed by horror. You can "sequester" the emotional trauma, the torture, the fear, like an oyster sequesters grit in a pearl. The MPD walls off a person, a personality. A strategy to partition the pain away from consciousness. How separate are these alternate personalities? I mean, we all have separate personalities. When you talk to your mother you are a different person then you are when you talk to your friends. When you are alone in bed at night you are a different person again. But these different personalities share memories. Not so the MPD's "alters". They are walled off: "sequestered". Alters have even been documented with allergies not shared by the other personalities. They are, to all intents and purposes, separate people.

It's a sign that something may be going on, writes Dr. Putnam, when you find cloths in your closet that you don't recognize.

"You can't imagine how strange it is," said Jus, "to wake and wonder how the flat-screen television got there. To wake up in your boarding house room and wonder where you are and how you got there."

Why was I so fond of Jus? He was pleasant with me, considerate, and I considered him a hero in his way, that he would now embrace his pain to mend such hurt. And he seemed fond of me and he was ever so respectful.

So we worked with Jus' rib, and then we worked with Jus. We? Me and mostly Jus himself. I rarely met his alters.

Jus' story. Justin Coffin's father was a Satanist, Jus told me. There is a hotbed of Satanists on Vancouver Island. It's the satanic capital of Canada.

"What about the Ottawa valley?" I asked.

"Oh yeah, but Vancouver Island's the place."

If you swear allegiance to the Devil, Jus swears, the Devil will give you anything you want... in the short term. But you have to seal the deal with blood – not your high school slash your finger blood. No. The blood of a relative, and all their blood. A murder, perhaps of your child. Then the Devil will give you millions of dollars, or sex, or power. Whatever you want, and quick. There are quite a few, true, Satanists, though there are a lot more low-grade imitators and dabblers too.

One of the reasons Jus trusted me, and worked with me, was to do with an incident that happened around that time, that I related to him in the context of getting things by just asking. I'd come across a Buddhist sect – the Nichiren Buddhists – many of whose followers claimed that if you said their mantra and asked for something, the universe would deliver. So I asked for a new patient: "Nam myoho renge kyo": and the phone rang. And then it range again. That didn't feel quite right, so I stopped saying the mantra. And because of that, Jus trusted me.

Jus' story: continued... Jus was a victim of severe childhood abuse. "Here, look at this scar. My father hammered a nail through my hand just there. Nailed me to the table. Some times he'd put me in a freezer, with the power off, but pitch dark, for hours on end. I used to like that. That's when Jesus would come to me, and take over. Just a calm black void and bliss. Safe."

"Was Jesus one of your alters?"

"At times. When I was a kid. When I was safe."

Multiple Personality is a strategy for the overwhelmed, the tortured. "When I was eleven years old my Pa put a gun in my mouth and made me fuck my mother."

Torture. You may want to skip the next two paragraphs. On Halloween the Satanists convene for their high mass. "Yeah, they'll sacrifice some babies. But more are offered to the devil for possession. It's an honor to offer a child to the master for him to possess. They only do this with kids till they're six years old. So, so this happened to me once a year till I was six." They would fuck me, fuck the child - the congregation would bugger, or fuck, the child - until 'it left its body.' Then they'd call in a spirit to take possession."

"I can remember leaving my body, hovering up near the

ceiling, in the corner, and watching them bugger me. And they know when you leave your body. I watched them call the spirits in. Saw the devils entering my body. I have six entities that share my body, that still possess me. One of them, the last one they called in, is the Devil himself."

Jus' father died when Jus was fourteen. "He buried something before he died. Buried something in a chest in the woods. I met an Indian medicine man not long ago. A wise and powerful man. He said that chest is important. That I need to retrieve it. To open it. I'm trying to get the courage to go out to B.C. and do that. But it frightens me."

It took a while for Jus to find that courage. Meanwhile he came to see me. I do a lot of CranioSacral Therapy which is deeply relaxing and can be transformative in many ways: physically, emotionally, psychologically, spiritually. And though I didn't often see Jus Coffin "switch", nor meet many of his alters, I did meet some.

Once, a man that looked very like Jus, but with a quite different demeanor, arrived for his appointment. A much gruffer dude introduced himself. "I'm Jude. I'm one of Jus' protective personalities." In a deep, hoarse voice he explained that just before arriving Jus had witnessed a couple arguing, fighting, and though the woman was giving her partner more grief then she was getting, Jus had quite a "thing" about men abusing women, his mother having been so sorely used. So he switched and Jude laid the poor fellow out cold with a couple of punches. He had bruised his hand some. Would I do acupuncture for it, he asked. I gave him some homeopathic arnica, but sure, acupuncture could certainly dull the pain and probably speed up the healing. "Do you enjoy sticking needles into people?" he asked

"Not particularly."

"Me, I like hurting people," he said pounding the injured fist into his palm. "They should know what it feels like," he said grimly.

"I'm going to put a couple of needles in your hands in Hoku for the pain," I told him. "And one in your head, Baihui, to calm you down."

Baihui is amazing. My teacher, Jayasuaria, calls it "the Valium point". When I needled Baihui, Jude's eyes flickered. He twitched and switched back into Jus. "I hope Jude didn't scare you."

Jus told me that he and Dr. Mann had uncovered two homicides, and he feared there might have been more; lowlifes he had fallen in with, who had tried to cheat him some. A dumb move. Jus felt they had it coming, but he was also remorseful. Part of the reason he now wanted to heal. As I've said, I viewed his attempts at integration and redemption as quite heroic.

At this time Jus moved to a room in a new rooming house. Moving in he felt unease. Though the walls had been painted white since the last occupant, he could sense Satanic designs, graffiti, that the last occupant had painted: he was sure he sensed or saw this under the new paint. And there was a lingering smell of demonic candles. "They use black candles with human fat in them. Human fat, or in pinch a black cat's, though you can smell the difference."

Jus asked if I thought I could "clean" the room. He said his Indian medicine man had said that I could. I wasn't brimming with confidence about this, but I said I would try next week, when I got back from Blue Skies. Blue Skies is the most wonderful of folk music festivals. Only two thousand folk can camp there. That's what the field, the space, would sustainably support, so the tickets are allotted by lottery and the community is the cream of what would be the "counter culture" if the counter culture were still alive. (And it probably is. It's us old liberals.)

At Blue Skies I met a young man with a sound grounded presence, though he called himself a white magician, a wizard, and a "shaman", and only the last in quotation marks, because, as he explained, "I'm not a Siberian. I mostly trained with the Lakota." Nonetheless, for all these words, I still had a good feeling about Tim and I asked him for his advice about cleansing Jus' room. Tim gave me a formula wherein I would call on all the entities, forces, powers (an inclusive list) that were not "pure" and dancing in the light, to leave and stay away. It was in a sort of spiritual lawyer's language and I can only paraphrase, for I can't, now, find the text.

I told Tim I was a little tremulous about ordering the spirits gone in my own name. Couldn't I do it in Jesus' name, or some great dude?

Tim said, "When you go into that room you are going to be the most powerful presence there. You just order them gone. They'll go. But you've got to dot your "i"s and cross your "t"s, cause they're squirmy. They are literalists and they are looking for loopholes."

I smudged Jus' room with cedar. I smudged it with sage and sweet grass. I said the formula with steadfast conviction. And we smudged a can of paint for Jus to paint again.

Later Jus told me that when I had smudges him, he could feel the entities in him, the Devil and demons, shrink away from the smoke. They did not like it. They had a power over him, particularly the "Devil" did. He would reward Jus for doing things he wanted with orgasmic paroxysms. Jus, and most of his alters, could resist the "Devil's" urgings easily enough, but the rewards had some allure.

And the smudged, cleansed room? Better, but Jus was never comfortable there.

Then Jus was gone a while. Months later he came back to my practice. He'd been to B.C. Had dug up his father's chest. Nothing of importance in it. A let down.

Jus had told me how once in therapy with Dr. Mann, he had changed, like a werewolf, into a hyena headed creature. Literally, Dr. Mann had fled the room, he said.

Dr. Mann, said Jus, was trying to arrange for an exorcism. He had corresponded with, and talked with, a branch of the Church, a Vatican committee that dealt with such stuff, and they were working on it, the bell, book and candle thing, but… but there was a lot of paper work, bureaucracy, and training. They were meeting with Jus. Had been meeting with him to prepare him but they had told him it would take a long time to prepare him, before he was ready. Perhaps a year. (Did he have to repent all his sins before they would begin?)

At this time, and this will date it for me -1994, '95 – I was working with a spiritual healer, R.D. R.D. would come to my office Wednesday evenings to treat her patients, and some of mine. I had seen her work with "possession", exorcising entities (though half the time that she was asked to do this, she discerned rather that the person asking was delusional – that it was "all in their head"). I asked Jus if he was interested in meeting R.D., and they arranged to work together.

R.D. talked with the entities, dialogued with them one by one, inviting them, guiding, facilitating their leaving. It seems that ghosts or entities that take possession of people (usually people who are in some degree incapacitated, so you'll find these hungry ghosts hanging out in bars, for drunks, and hospitals, waiting on their chances, or so Tim the "shaman" told me), these entities are souls in dread of passing on, fearing hell fires. R.D. explained to them that it wasn't like that. That Earth is a school and our lives are lessons, and it wasn't fire and brimstone they'd earned as the wages for their sins, but remedial classes: come back and try again, and she'd convince them to leave. Well, it took the first hour's session to convince the first three. The next two traveled on easily, quickly, in the next session, but the "Devil" was hard to move. He was hanging on for dear life. They talked at length. R.D. would speak and then listen. Finally she arrived at a tactic that began to make an impact. "You don't want that body," she cajoled; playfully, but disdainfully, she taunted him. She explained to me later that this sixth entity was quite a dandy. He'd been hanging round in one body, then another, for decades - an Edwardian dandy – and he was indeed mortified to be confined in such a low class person, body builder though Jus was in those days, and quite a handsome man. It was this disparagement of Jus as an unsuitable host that finally did the trick. The Devil (he called himself the Devil to Jus. To R.D. he was Damien)… Damian was, actually quite bored, and he decided he might journey on.

"Look over there, by the willow tree." R.D. eyes glanced over to, and through, the corner of the room. "Those three angels. They're here to guide you… No. No, they're not here to punish or confine you. They just look like angels. That's how you picture them. They're spirits. They have no form, no real form… Over there by the tree, by the stream. They're waiting."

"Well, Jus," I asked when he came to see me next, "do you feel deferent? Did it work?"

Jus wasn't sure. "But it was sure weird. You only heard one side of the conversation. I heard both sides!"

Jus said he still felt the devil in him. R.D. insisted the Devil, Damien, had left and that Jus was just so used to the shape of him that he felt him still. And, she thought, Jus still desired Damien's strength and power in some degree.

Jus felt he was still possessed.

How do I know any of this is true? Jus once showed me a copy of a letter Dr. Mann had written to the church council concerning the possible Church exorcism they were planning. (I later met Dr. Mann in connection with another patient and he was indeed head of psychiatry at McPherson's.) Written on McPherson Hospital letterhead the letter went on to describe Dr. Mann's conviction that something unworldly was indeed happening (he had to convince them that it really was "demonic possession" and not just delusions). He wrote that he had seen Jus' visage change physically into a wolf's head.

"It wasn't a wolf," Jus said, with distain, as I read. "It was a hyena, and besides, how would he know. He ran out of the room when I started to switch."

The third year I was working with Jus, for the changes were slow and while his work with Dr. Mann was steady, his work with me was intermittent… the third year he was no longer a fit bodybuilder. He had run to pudge… he was pudgy and he'd become a little sallow. (Well, he was haunted.) He was now living with a sweet, sweet woman, Jenny Hu. She came to sessions with him a few times. Spoke with an accent. Worked for bell Telephone. A slightly built, attractive woman, and so caring. She doted on Jus. But Jus was doubtful about the relationship: felt that it wasn't good for Jenny. Some of his alters, Jake and Jordan, were rude to her. He feared for her.

My final chapter with Jus involved the "healer", R.D., again. R.D. was then a student film maker. She wanted to make a "short" about Justin the Multiple for her film course. A documentary. He agreed. On camera he changed and switched, and switched: mostly babies and toddlers. With the older of these he'd talk in a silly baby voice. "I'm Jimmy. I'm a good boy." With the younger, he'd "goo" and "gah" and dribble. Vulnerable innocent infants. Sad. I'd not seen any of this before with Jus.

I was rather conflicted about this documentary project that we shot at my office. It felt a little exploitive, unfeeling, to me and I feared it might tarnish Jus and my "therapeutic relationship", even though it was not, directly, my project. It might have been difficult for me to veto. That would have needed some balls, and I was "conflicted". I don't know if Jus, or any of his alters, also felt this disquiet. It was the last that I saw of Justin Coffin.

PIP'S CHOICE

Pip set out in November. He had three thousand dollars, U.S., in travelers cheques and one hundred dollars cash. He drove down to Windsor, hit the casino, and won three thousand Canadian on the slots. Night in a five star hotel. In his recollection, a fabulous meal. Drove on the Chicago, to Herod's River Boat Casino. Won thirty three hundred, American. He went to a second river boat casino and won another two thousand. He drove down to St. Louis. Lost a thousand. In Kansas City he had an oil change and a truck stop lunch; pork chops, fried chicken, mash, green beans, salad, the best meal he'd ever had. Drove down to Oklahoma City. Lost a thousand. In Albuquerque he stayed at the El Rancho Hotel and he did quite well. He gambled for three days and only lost a thousand dollars. Visiting a casino in Flagstaff he lost another thousand. Hit Los Vegas, the Barbary Coast Hotel on the strip. Won seven or eight hundred. At Bali's he won a thousand. In Caesar's Palace he lost two or three thousand. But his stocks were up. He went back to Caesar's Palace and lost another two thousand, and that sort of cleaned him out.

Pip drove across Death Valley. "I think I came on this trip to die," he told himself. He crossed the mountains, Sacramento, San Francisco, turned north across the Golden Gate Bridge. He put his feet in the Pacific and drove on northwards. In Portland he called his brother in Toronto. His brother, David, flew out to meet him in Vancouver. They drove over the Rockies to Banff. Another wonderful hotel. Hot springs. Another wonderful meal. (Actually, as Pip recalled the story to me there was extraordinary meal after extraordinary meal, but I've left most out for brevity.) In Calgary Pip lost a thousand dollars of David's money. Past Kenora in western Ontario on the way to Soiux Ste. Marie the road feels mountainous. A huge truck carrying timber was approaching them on the mountain road and suddenly some fool was trying to pass it. There was no room for the three of them. "We're going to die," thought Pip.

"Just as I suspected." But they didn't. They squeezed past and drove home to Toronto

.   "The worst thing about it all," said Pip, "was that I knew I'd have to tell you and tell my therapist." But that's not the point of the story. The point of the story, the bit I felt was poignant was that when Pip was driving out of Chicago with ten thousand dollars in his pocket, he was faced with the choice, ("Faced again with the choice," he says) of turning right, west, and driving to Pipestone, Minnesota, to buy up some pipestone, and then maybe looking for Leonard Crow Dog in the Dakotas - chasing spirit - or turning south and following his addiction. And we do it all the time... I do it all the time, eat that chocolate, that French-fry, that cigarette. Why is the downward path the path of least resistance? Potential energy and gravity. "Well," say Pip, lying "I turned south because it was turning cold."

SYMPTOMS (AN INTRODUCTION)

Soon after my marriage (and life) fell apart, I was driving down to Brighton with my father. He passed on the advise (oh, then, and again, and again) "Make notes. Take notes." My father was a writer.

"Have you thought of writing?" he asks his dropped-out son.
"Yes," I said, "but what?"
"You must have a story?"
Hesitantly, "Well I do"
"Tell me the story. I'll work with you on it. I'll edit it."
I told Ted my story. "Write it as a T.V. drama. An hour." We worked through six drafts, and he liked the seventh. He had molded some of story for me. Focused some on the father/son relationship. Showed me how to exaggerate and strategize judiciously. But, as you'll see, the subject matter doesn't really lend itself to television.

Years later I showed "Symptoms" to a T.V. producer, Martin Kinch, and he suggested, "If you write it as a stage play you can always arrange to get a reading."

Never happened. Not my forte. Then one day I thought, "Oh, I know," these decades later, "I'll rewrite it as a short story."

Oh, and generally speaking, I don't write "fiction"; I write "reportage", except for *Symptoms.* Under Ted's guidance we accentuated Martin's failings, and his relationship with his mother and father, to the point of fiction.

SYMPTOMS

ONE

There are many candled burning, but no other light, in this basement apartment room up near the Seven Dials. Martin has come to the séance as a skeptic. Really, he is just fascinated with Maggie. He thinks she is very pretty, in a masculine way, and he finds her ever so sexy. For the girls, Maggie and her flat-mates, the séances is a game, an amusement, though for Annie it will soon become more serious.

On the table, near the middle of the room, pieces of cardboard have been arranged in a circle as a Ouija board, numbers and letters and a "yes" and "no" . There's a small inverted glass tumbler in the middle of the circle which acts as an *indicator* to channel the spirits. Martin and the three girls have their fingers on the tumbler, the indicator, as it flits among the letters. Martin wonders if he is part of the "medium". Peter, Martin's friend, records the letters as Jenny calls them out. "I, W, O, R, R, Y, 4, U, R, M, O, H, E, R," recites Jenny.

Jenny is a pretty, a sparkling girl. She's a hippy. It's 1969. Hippy is *a la mode*. Maggie will pass for a hippy too. Her hair is long and dark. Annie, the third flat-mate, is homelier. "A northern lass, without much class," Maggie might say to be cruel.

The room is candle lit. It is a basement apartment. The walls are flickering shadows. There are mirrors on the walls. The girls have hung them to watch their hair glow. There is also psychedelia: Fillmore Hall postures, red green op art flashing. The furniture is cheap - junk shops rather than antique shops - the futon, though, is new.

Peter reads, "I worry for your mother." Peter, the fifth member of the party, is twenty three, relatively "straight" to look at, but his flexible mind shows on his face. He does not cut an exciting figure. He's serious and, in a quiet way, he's efficient with everything he does. He jots down his notes with a precise hand.

The tumbler hesitates, then rushes between the letters. "A, R, I, N, G, Q," Jenny calls. The indicator then pauses before bouncing back and forth between the A and Q, gravitating towards and circling the letter Q. (A, Q, R, A, Q, A, Q, Q, Q.)

Annie is stricken, ashen. Agitated, she gets up from the table. "I must go a ring Da. Excuse me." She grabs her scarf and bag and leaves.

"It is iver ever over now," Peter reads. "I worry for "you-are" mother. "A" ring Q. A Q." Jenny explains that Anne's father is in hospital. "Heart attack. She thinks he's dying. It's a Queensbury number."

"Not the best time to be dabbling with the occult," says Martin.

"Au contraire," says Maggie. "It's the most perspicuous time to tap psychic energies." There is a tinge of hostility there.

Martin dodges her stare. "Do you think the three of us are enough to keep the tumbler turning?"

"We can but try," Maggie darts. They reach out for the tumbler. Martin, as before, stretches out with his right arm. He groans. "Ooh! Man, this is a strain."

"Only 'cause you're tense," says Jenny.

Martin stretches his neck and shoulder, raising his shoulder, bending his head into the pain. "In the neck, as it were. I've been switching arms all evening. I wonder if my left hand knows what my right hand's been saying?" He smiles. He's almost pleased with himself. He shakes and flexes his right arm and shoulder and switches to his left hand.

During this performance of Martin's, Jenny and Peter evince no interest, but Maggie is "bugged".

They prepare to start again. Jenny asks the ethers, "Is there anybody there?"

The tumble moves to "yes".

"Do you have a message for us?"

The tumbler flies back and forth between A and Z.

"A, Z, A, Z, A, Z," Jenny recites.

It stops.

"Alpha and Omega," pronounces Martin. "The beginning and the end. Everything and nothing." This engenders a pause.

Peter scans back through his notes. "Looks like everyone's had a message, except Martin."

"I'm happy," says Martin.

"Oh, no," says Maggie. "We must have something special for Martin." In a theatrical voice she addresses the airs. "Spirits! Spirits! Ghouls and giests, could we please have a message for Martinkipooh."

The tumbler starts to move. Jenny, Martin, Maggie have their fingers on the glass: however, this time it appears to Martin that Maggie is blatantly, consciously, pushing the tumbler.

Jenny calls out, "D R O P D E A..."

"Drop dead," says Martin blandly. With some resentment he accuses Maggie, "You pushed it."

"The spirit moved me," she says like ice.

Jenny jumps to her feet. "Coffee?"

It is later in the evening. The sitting-room doubles as Maggie's bedroom at one end, her futon spread on the floor. At the other end of the room there is a thorough-fare to the kitchen from the rest of the flat, the basement apartment that Maggie shares with Jenny and Annie. The room now is lit, side-lit by table lamps and a floor lamp. Maggie's bed is at the south end of the room. Maggie and Martin are sitting on the bed. Martin is twenty four years old, a graduate student. He is a tall lad, good looking, long hair. He could have been a very impressive figure, but he lacks the confidence.

At the table, at the north end of the room, Peter and Jenny are comforting Annie. Annie is distressed. Between the table and the bed there is a sofa and an armchair. And the stereo. The music on the stereo is the Beach Boys' "Holland". One of "the hundred inevitables," Maggie would say. "Sail on sail on sailor," sing the Beach Boys. "The album is hauntingly out of character for the Beach Boys," Martin would say. "It's blithe."

"Maggie, love?" asks Martin.

Maggie answers archly. "Martin, darling,"

"Do you still want to trip on Tuesday?"

Maggie is irritated. "Today is Friday. Tomorrow's Saturday. Sunday follows that. Then comes Monday. Come round Tuesday, if you like. We'll see how we feel. I can't give you more then that. You'll just have to wait and see."

TWO

Another day: Martin sits in a plush leather chair in his father office, waiting. For Martin the office presents some contradictions. It has a spacious old world authority, and an authoritarian claustrophobia. Martin watches the dust motes lit by the sunlight through the high narrow windows. He always finds this creates an experience of "presence", if he's present enough to experience it. "Be here," tells himself. It's his mantra for the week.

His father, Dr. Howard, is a leading Thoracic Surgeon at a London teaching hospital. Martin Howard, the son has come up from Brighton where he lives, where he is working on his Ph.D. (Well, it's a D. Phil. at Sussex. Sussex is modeled on Oxford so it's a "D.Phil." not a "Ph.D.") Martin's doctoral thesis is in psychology; medicines poor cousin.

Martin has taken the train up from Brighton, taken tea in the Pullman car, one of the little luxuries Amy's working as a teacher affords him beyond his graduate's grant. Amy is Martin's wife. Maggie is his mistress. Martin is modeling on his father, Professor Julian Howard. Julian is a larger than life figure. Friend of royalty, TV personality, authority on all things medical. Womanizer, though now with "trophy wife".

The door handle turns. The door is set ajar. Professor Howard voice comes through the door. "No. You can make your incision very low at the side, here... and come up to it from underneath. I'll try to sit in."

"Thank you, Sir," says a voice.

"Let my secretary know when and where you're operating." Professor Howard enters his office. He is tall, white haired, suave. "Oh, hello, Martin. And what brings you to our great grey Metropolis?"

"I had some research to do at the British Museum, so, as I was just round the corner, I thought I'd honour my father."

"Well, I'm very pleased you did. We don't see enough of you nowadays... Have you seen your mother? She's phoned me twice this week, you know, to ask if I know how you're getting on." Professor Howard sorts through the papers on his desk. His attention is split, not fully with his son. "You know, Martin, it really wouldn't hurt you to phone her now and then. She worries about you. Phone her up, oh, say once a week, and just tell her 'everything's going fine'. That way she'll leave us alone."

Martin grins. He does not expect any real communication with his father, but he is enjoying the show. The good Doctor, abstracted, continues. "I wish you wouldn't provide her with an excuse to keep pestering me. You phone her. I pay a very handsome alimony to keep her out of my hair."

"Well, son," says the Doctor in a "that's that" voice, confident that these matters are settled and we all agree so now let's change the subject. "How's your Ph.D. thesis progressing? I still wish you'd taken a medical degree. It's not too late... Hmm. You and Amy must come up soon and spend and evening with Angela and I. Angela's often asking after you. We could go out to the theatre. Oh, I forgot. You don't like the theatre. And you don't have a television. What do you and Amy do with yourselves for amusement?"

THREE

Brighton sleeps. Martin is awake. He sits up in his bedroom, in his bed, writing intently in a small notebook. He glances down at his side at his wife, who is sleeping beside him. Amy is twenty seven with a pretty and interesting face. "Your hair upon the pillow like a sleepy golden storm," thinks Martin, quoting Leonard Cohen's then current album. Another of "the hundred inevitable" Maggie would say. Martin focuses back on his writing and reads to himself softly, aloud, this evening's poem. It's about Maggie, his obsession.

"First I free you. Then I tighten the rope and strangle an image of you, freeze an image, a form, fixed form, formless; embodiment of my body want, formless. Ice melting into damp, heat flaring into screaming, leaving me unwarmed, unchanged, unmoved - damp, fearful, small, but unquenched, with winter's wants and winter's words set to begin the same again before the early dusk brings the same dark."

Martin is pleased with his poem and so, though he feels dark, he is also grimly pleased with himself, again. Smug. "What's it mean?" he whispers. He lies back and closes his eyes.

He drifts into reverie. He sees Maggie's face approaching him. She's cackling like a witch. She draws near. Her laughter becomes less and less devilish, becomes neutral, neither malicious nor merry.

Behind Maggie there is an open doorway. It leads into a church. A large empty space. It's a barn of a church, very dim. As Martin walks slowly over to the pulpit he begins to recite: "Before time began I lay and dreamt..." In front of Martin, in his dream, there is an altar with a casket. Candles around it. Martin sees himself laid out in a coffin. Amy, his wife, Maggie, his mistress, his father, Professor Howard stand over the coffin, mourning. Behind them a veiled woman stands in the shadows.

"*I don't like the look of this,*" thinks Martin. The body in the casket, the corpse Martin, rises in its shroud. It walks towards Martin. Walks through Martin. Martin's dream reverie segues to…

Martin, in Renascence dress, lying under a willow tree by a stream. He mouths a blade of grass and recites, "Before time began I lay and dreamt, of all the conquest, all the glory…" Maggie rises from the river, a water nymph, dressed only in a towel, and with a towel round her head. Dream Martin continues his recitation, "… all the wonder of the world, and woke…"

Maggie is in front of a doorway. She is laughing. Her laughter starts neutral, as before, but quickly evolves into a enchanting child-like giggle.

"…and woke to find…"

Maggie turns and walks through the doorway, swinging the door closed behind her, but before it quite closes, it's closing again, it's closing again, as Martin completes his recitation…

"… the ever closing door."

Martin dreams that he is awake looking out of the living-room window onto Palmeira Square. He is watching himself.

Palmeira Square is a pseudo-Georgian (Victorian) "square" in Brighton landscaped down to the sea. Grand. Old.

Martin and Amy are waking in the square, in the park, hand in hand. Amy says, "Your mother called."

Martin wakes with a start. His eyes are large. His heart is racing. He can almost hear it, his heart. He can certainly feel it. He stares at the ceiling. Then he gets out of bed. He is naked. He goes to the kitchen. Prepares a bowl of muesli. He walks through to the living-room, looks on the darkened square munching his muesli.

. He hears the dawn chorus - sparrows chattering, starling shrieking. He hears the clink of a milk float Otherwise it is very quiet. Martin feels quiet alone. He sighs and recites, "And woke to find the ever closing door."

FOUR

Martin and Amy are walking in the park outside their Palmeira Square flat. They walk hand in hand. Martin fingers Amy's wedding ring. Feels its round unfaceted emerald. It's a wide silver band. *"My marriage band. A cheap but beautiful antique. My marriage vows. Amo, amas, amat…"* His mind is far away… from everything. Amy's voice interrupts… "Your mother called."

Martin's face briefly registers surprise and shock. This is *"deja vu"* of his recent dream and he's not sure, for a moment, whether he's awake or asleep. He lets go of Amy's hand and puts his hands in the back pockets of his jeans. He frowns. The square frowns back.

Amy repeats, "Your mother phoned."

Martin collects himself and answers glibly, "She asked the usual. You told her the usual. You said I was fine."

They walk on in silence. Amy bends down and picks up a leaf. She looks at it as they walk along. She holds it out for Martin. He shows no sign of noticing or responding to the gesture. Amy is disappointed. "Are you fine?" she asks.

Martin stops. "I'm confused. I have been tangled in an obsession with Maggie. It's over. I'll be fine next week. That's a promise." He reaches out for, and takes, her hands. "Just indulge me for a few more days. I know you're impatient." He moves closer to her. "But I also know that everything's going to work out fine." He whirls Amy around, "because you, little lady, are my guardian angel."

They both smile briefly. Martin is very proud that he can talk about these things. None the less, his smile is sheepish. Amy's smile is long-suffering. "Don't count on it," she says.

They pass a young couple billing and cooing on a park bench. Martin and Amy feel the contrast - they can't miss it - between the couple's hope and enthusiasm and Martin's sad contortions. They walk on, no longer hand in hand. They come to a spot where one of the tall trees in the square has been cut down and sawn into logs. "Look. Isn't that sad?" says Amy.

Martin kneels to study one of the logs. "Yeah. Look at the colours on the bark! They're fantastic?" Vivid greens and purples on contrasting grays and blacks. "I'd like to take one home."

"Why?" asks Amy.

"I don't know. I just fancy it." Martin fancies of himself as a lumberjack chopping at some tall pine tree - though these logs are sycamore. In his fantasy he is lugging his pine tree, a Christmas tree, home through the snow. "Why?" he repeats. "To preserve it a while. I don't know. Maybe it's just a wooden attempt at eccentricity." "*A wooden pun,*" thinks Martin. The grey bark of the sycamore flakes off in a contoued patterning. "I'll pick it up on the way home," he concludes.

Martin and Amy amble down to the beach. They look out at the grey sea and sky. It's a pebble beach. The surf's undertow rattles and roars rhythmically. Martin points upward, away from the noise, with his left hand. "Look there!"

Overhead a large flock of ducks is flying in several small "v"ed groups. Martin keeps pointing skyward. *"The ducks are writing patterns in the sky," he thinks.* "Nature is writing secrets everywhere." He opens his hand and with his arm still extended he makes an expansive, inclusive gesture to accompany his "everywhere." Suddenly he is stricken. Obviously in great pain, he drops his left arm, grabs at his left pectoral muscles (with his right-hand) and collapses his shoulders forward

"What's wrong?" asks Amy. "What is it?"

Martin is in considerable, but diminishing pain, yet has difficulty speaking. " Oh, man. I've got this sudden... burning... pain in my chest and shoulder... I think we'd better start back."

They walk briskly back towards home, as briskly as they can with Martin drooping and favouring his shoulders. They pass by the log Martin has coveted earlier. *"Later,"* he thinks. "Shit," he lisps.

FIVE

Martin is in the sitting room. He is doing a sort of Indian war-dance with little skipping steps, gesturing with his right hand to ward off the evil eye. His left arm hangs limp. Amy comes into the sitting room and looks on with good humoured amazement.

"What on earth are you doing?"

Martin is in a good humour too. He does not take himself seriously. "Someone's trying to put a curse on me. I'm fighting it."

"Who?"

Martin puts his hand to his mouth and whispers, "People."

The phone rings. Martin is startled. He redoubles his war-dance as Amy goes off to the phone.

Martin puts a record on the stereo. The Rolling Stones "Between the Buttons". *"Another of the hundred inevitable,"* thinks Martin. He dances crazy awhile. A puzzled expression arrives on his face. He walks up the corridor to the bathroom. Amy is just getting into the bath. Martin peeks his head round the door. "Who was that on the phone?"

"It was for me."

Martin goes back into his shuffling, skipping war-dance as he enters the bathroom. "It's working," he says.

"Wow!" says Amy. "You really are scared of your mother. Do you think she rides a broom stick..."

"Yes, and she'll sweep down the phone line, pop out of the receiver..." Martin makes a sort of breast-stroke emerging, leafing-through-the-undergrowth gesture and then shakes his

116

fist in his own face. "...pop out of the receiver and clean me up."

"What are you frightened of?"

"It's not that I'm scared. It's just she's always getting at me." Martin runs the hot water into the basin to shave, and continues, "Subtly putting me down. 'When are you going to get your hair cut?' Mind you, there's nothing subtle about that." He splashes water onto his face. "Yes, I am scared of her. I do think she's a witch. She's still got cuttings of my baby hair!" Then he turns to Amy in the middle of lathering his face. "I wish you wouldn't see her."

"Look," says Amy, "she's his monster. She's your mumster. She's not my monster. She's got no-one. Someone's got to see her."

"Poor little old lady," says Martin.

"She's you mother."

"When I grew up, I left home."

Martin starts to shave. He raises his left hand to manipulate his cheek, but he finds that he cannot raise it higher then shoulder height. "I can't raise my arm."

The telephone rings down the hall. "Could you answer it?" asks Martin.

"I just got into the bath! What! Are you that paralyzed ?"

"It's not paralysis. It's principle."

Amy gives an exasperated sigh and gets up and out of the bathtub. Martin continues shaving. After he has finished and rinsed his face, he walks down the hallway wiping his face with a towel. Amy, in a towel, is on her way back to the bath. "It was your father," she says in passing. "He asked me to remind you to phone your mother."

Later the same evening, Amy is in the kitchen chopping vegetables. Martin has just nipped out for a minute - no, he didn't phone Maggie - he nipped over to the Off License to get some beer. Now he's back, closing the front door behind him, walking up to the kitchen carrying a couple of brown quart bottles. He arrives in the kitchen, grunts, and goes over to the stove. He picks

up the wooden spoon to sample Amy's vegetable stew. *"Il et ya besoin du plus de garlic!"* he says with a rather pseudo French accent.

"Your mother phoned again," Amy segues casually.

"Ho ho, she's persistent. What'd she want?"

Amy screws up her brow in mock concentration. "Let's see. 'How are you? How's my son? Are you feeding him properly? Is he getting enough protein?' "

"Yeah. She distrusts vegetarians more than homosexuals."

" 'Did he get the sweater I sent?' You really should have thanked her."

Martin snorts, "Mmf!" Amy continues, "Oh, yes, and she invited me to the Swedish Bazaar next week."

"You're not going with her, surely?"

"Well, I think I might. I can pick up a lot of useful Christmas presents. We get on well together, your mother and I."

Martin winces. Now he sits down on the floor in the corner. This action accompanies and, to some extent masks, his next words. "Do you think she really likes you?"

"Pardon," Amy asks.

"I said, 'Do you think that she really likes you?' "

"She's nice to me. That's usually an indication."

"She sees you to get to me!"

There's a pause. Then Amy asks, "Martin?"

"Yes."

"Do you like me?"

"I know it's hard to believe the way I've been carrying on of late, but at the deepest most profound levels I really truly love you. We'll grow into each other."

Amy throws the last of the veggies into the casserole. "That explains it."

"What?"

"Why it's at the surface, most superficial levels that it hurts."

The electric kettle has started to boil. Amy fills a large saucepan from the kettle and brings it over to the stove where she stands holding it. It is heavy. "Could you move the casserole onto the back ring for me?" she asks.

Martin gets up and comes over to the stove. He moves the casserole using his right hand only, favouring his left, and this proves awkward. Eventually Amy gets to put down the saucepan. "You're like Humpty Dumpty fretting over his fall," she says. "Don't you think you'd better see a doctor?" Amy opens a packet of spaghetti, puts the pasta into the water, and stirs.

"Yes," says Martin. "I will. I'll see Dr. Griffin tomorrow. But I'm sure it's only a strained muscle, so I'm a bit apprehensive about taking it to Griffin." Martin sits again on the floor in the corner. "Remember last spring when I had that lump in my ear. They're always telling you how a lump can be cancer and there's only hope if they catch it soon enough. So I went along to the clinic and the Sister said it was only a sebaceous cyst. So, I said, 'thank you', but she said, 'if you're at all worried you can see the doctor', and I said, 'no, that's alright, not to bother', but she went on insisting. Anyway, I thought, if I'm going to bother the doctor about the cyst, I might as well ask him about the other little medical matters on my mind, like that patch of dead skin on my foot, one inch in the grave, and the grunge between my toes which isn't quite Athlete's Foot, me not being an Athlete, and Griffin says to me, 'What is far more interesting than these symptoms, is why you bring them to me.' I didn't bring them for your entertainment. I brought them because the bloody nurse insisted, you silly old fart!"

Martin gets up and Amy says, "You told that very well, but enjoyed it more when it was current. I guess it was the novelty."

"Oh, did I tell you all that before? I didn't remember…"

Amy hugs him, with genuine affection. Martin is a little baffled, and remains remote. He starts feeling his chest. "I'll ask Dr. Griffin about my heart, too. It feels a bit funny. Must be linked with the shoulder strain. I hope it doesn't stop me tripping with Maggie on Tuesday. You know I told her I'd "trip-guide" her. I want to get that one out of the way. Free myself from her. Resolve things. Once and for all."

Amy heaves a resigned sigh.

SIX

Martin is stripped to the waist. Dr. Griffin is examining his shoulder. Dr. Griffin is small, slim, distinguished looking and gentle spoken. Martin, is in a light mood. He is flexing his shoulder, and he comments, "Then I shouldn't play squish..." It's a genuine slip of the tongue. He corrects himself, "Squash?"

"No squish or squash," says Dr. Griffin. "No heavy lifting. There's no need for medication, but be sure you rest it for a few days."

Martin continues with a further inquiry in a hesitant manner. "There's something else I wanted to mention. Since I strained the shoulder, I've been strangely aware of my heart. It feels... different, sort of as if it were beating against the chest wall."

"I'd better have a listen," says Dr. Griffin. He picks up his stethoscope. "I hope this isn't too cold. There." The doctor auscultates for a short while and then reassures Martin, "No, there's nothing wrong there. You're sound as a bell."

Martin starts to dress. "Yeah," he says. "It's just I've been aware of it almost continually. Strange? Still, if you say there's nothing to worry about... Mmm... is there any contraindication for cardiac stimulants?"

"Which stimulants?!"

"Oh, caffeine, nicotine. The usual."

"Here is always a contraindication for nicotine," says Griffin "but no." The doctor goes over to his desk. "The heart is actually a very robust organ. It can sustain a great deal of exertion. If it didn't, we wouldn't survive as a species." The doctor glances through Martin's file as he speaks. "The heart can maintain a rate of a hundred and eighty beats, two hundred beats a minute for several days and it would be none the worse. In someone of your age there's absolutely no cause for concern. Heart disease is still a disease of old age. Put it out of your mind."

Martin prepares to leave. "Well, thank you for your reassurance. Sorry to have troubled you."

Dr. Griffin looks up from Martin's file. "You seem to have a rather undue concern about your health. A degree of hypochondria. Perhaps you might like to arrange an appointment to discuss this problem?"

"Well, I'll think about it," says Martin, opening the door. "Thank you."

SEVEN

Martin's friend Peter's has a small cubbyhole of a laboratory-come-office in the Biology building. No windows. Peter is projecting a film onto his white walls, a film of microbes bumping together, having "sex" or the microbial equivalent thereof: an exchange of genetic material. Peter jots down the occasional note in the lab book on his lap. He takes his work seriously. This is the dawn of genetic engineering.

There is a knock at the door. "Come in," says Peter. Martin enters. "Oh, hello," says Peter. "Here, have you ever seen bugs making it? That's what you're watching. 'Conjugation', we call it." Peter is a much more stable personality than his friend

Martin but he can't help but envy what he thinks is Martin's "flair".

Martin musters some enthusiasm. "It looks fascinating. Yeah!" He pauses. "Peter, I won't be able to pay squash this afternoon."

"Oh?"

"I've strained my shoulder. It must have been the Ouija: holding my arm up for hours." Martin gestures with his right arm, weakly. "Dr. Griffin prescribes rest and psychotherapy." Peter rewards him with a chuckle. Martin continues, "I've got a curious heart symptom, too. I'm strangely aware of each beat."

"Well, that does sound psycho. Perhaps it's to tell you that you're in imminent danger of losing your heart altogether. You stand on the brink of heartbreak, Martin." Peter regards his friend quizzically. "You really are quite heartless."

"Me? Heartless?"

"I don't know why you protest. If I were Amy I'd have put you out to pasture long ago and found myself something with a seasoning of love and care."

During this speech it is Martin, now, who studies Peter with suspicion. "Mmm," says Martin. "No, Peter, I'm not heartless. I'm just powerless and confused. Hopeless, maybe. Ever since I trip-guided Maggie two months ago, I've been obsessed with her. I've got to work it out: work it through. Oh, that trip was so fantastic. 'Contact high', I guess. Perfect communion. She's so beautiful, and so alone."

Peter is disturbed listening to these things and gives his attention to the film. The film runs out, flutters, stutters and, for these moments, the projected square on the wall is a flickering white.

Martin notices that he has inadvertently upset his friend. He tries to soothe him. "There was nothing sexual about it, Peter. It's a head thing."

Peter switches the projector off and the lights on. "You had a 'scene' with her last spring, though, didn't you?"

"Yes. <u>Then</u> we were lovers. But it wasn't until she gave me up in the summer that I became fond of her. And then that trip, I fell in love… Shades of Carmen. Bad Karma, I know."

Peter changes the subject. "And how's your work coming along?"

"By degrees. 'The Patient's Conception of Schizophrenia', a complete madman's guide to insanity. When I started it seemed straight forward. Basically, you know, I was trying to develop the Laingian thesis that the schizophrenic is acting out a role given to him by his family. But the patients are all so confused. Most of them are drugged that madness is chemical, and of course chemistry is involved. Or they think it's congenital, sort of willed upon them by the new divinity of their spiraling DNA. Oh. A few of them perceive how their destruction is willed upon them in the actual in-fighting of family politics; the Hamlet thesis I'm trying to develop. But mostly, they won't cooperate." Martin smiles. "They're confused, and I'm getting confused too. 'Contact confusion'… No, the more I pursue my theories, the more they recede. All the connections keep breaking down, and I don't know where I am at all: not with my work and not with my women." Towards the end of his monologue Martin becomes uncomfortable and breaks into a "soft shoe routine". Then, feebly, he mimes a tennis stroke. "I can't play tennis. Anyone for lunch."

"Sure. I'll just tidy up."

Peter quickly straightens his domain. Martin watches Peter, stares at him. As Peter passes near to him to reach the door, Martin reaches his right arm to Peter's shoulder, arresting him. Peter turns. Martin drops his arm to say, "You know, Peter. You don't fool me."

"What do you mean by that?" They are face to face.

"You're after Amy. You wanted Maggie and you couldn't have her, and now you're making a play for Amy."

"Don't be ridiculous."

"You'll never find yourself," says Martin, "following me."

EIGHT

Across the road from the University, across the highway, is Falmer Station. A rustic little station. Maggie is walking towards the low brick building. The colour of the bricks a mix of grey and yellow. Black slate roof.

Martin has been running to catch up with her and is out of breath as he reaches her with an "Hello there." "Oh, hello," she says without enthusiasm. They hurry along the near side platform and across the foot bridge to the far platform. The Brighton train is coming.

"How are you?" asks Martin as they bustle along.

"About the same."

The train slows to a stop.

"How was your day?" asks Martin.

"About the same."

Martin opens a carriage door. He and Maggie board the train. Martin swings the door shut behind them. It closes with a clunk. "How's Anne's father?" he asks.

The train starts jerking Maggie forwards. "About the same," she answers.

Countryside and suburbia burn past the window. "He's not dead then?"

"No. He's about the same."

Martin studies Maggie's face. "And Jenny?" he asks.

Maggie is exasperated. "She's fine. Just fine."

"Has anything changed?"

"No. Everything's just about the same."

"And tomorrow?"

"What about tomorrow," Maggie asks.

"Do you want to trip?"

"About the same."

"Meaning?"

"Meaning 'we'll see' ".

The train rickety clatters into town. Martin and Maggie are silent. There is a long brickwork viaduct curving into the

124

station. It affords the passengers a panorama of the urban landscape, but Martin watches the floor.

The train rattles into the station with its grimy glass roof, and to a stop. Maggie and Martin join the crowd walking up the platform to the ticket collector's barrier. Martin hands in his ticket. Maggie stops and offers the ticket collector a five pound note. "Fourteen pence, please," she states.

The ticket collector speaks with a working-class argot: "'Ere, I ain't got that kinda change. How d'ja think you are?"

Maggie looks at him, dismisses him, and starts to walk away.

"'Ere, you! Come back 'ere!" The ticket collector takes a few quick strides after Maggie, apprehends her, laying hold of her shoulder.

"Take your hands off me, you great British oaf!" Maggie brushes off his hand with her hand and with the power of her disdain. But the Ticket Collector knows his due and his job.

"You can't ride the train without a ticket," he says. "What you think you're playing at?"

With a sneer Maggie offers him the fiver again.

The Ticket Collector is getting angry, and he counters with a, "Don't you get funny with me. You wait right there. I'll deal with you in a..."

"If you'll excuse me, constable, I'm in rather a hurry." She starts to walk off again.

The Ticket Collector loses his cool. Becomes nasty. "Bloody hippy! Little tramp!" He starts to pursue her.

Martin intervenes. "There's no need..." he begins.

"Dirty little tart!" the Ticket Collector spits, actually spits after her. He makes to push past Martin.

Martin spits in his face.

Both men are shocked and taken aback at this. Martin collects his wits and says mildly, "There's no cause to insult the young lady."

The Ticket Collector square himself to fight. Martin does likewise. The Ticket Collector is daunted and backs off. Then, turning to run, he shouts for assistance. ""Ere Fred! Agro."

Martin himself turns and runs after Maggie. Together they flee the station, cross the fore-court and without stopping, but with some caution, they run across the road and up the street. Up a steep hill and round a corner.

They are not being pursued. They slow down. Maggie is elated. She is skipping and hopping in childish delight. Martin, in contrast, is frightened and perturbed. "Buur," he shivers. "That really put the wind up me."

"What? That nice little man?"

"He spat at you and I spat in his face."

"Sir Galahad."

"All that violence," says Martin as though in shock.

"Perhaps you're a violent man, Martin."

"Oh, everyone's capable of aggression, but you pushed the buttons, and you revel in it." Maggie shrugs her shoulders. "You frighten me, Maggie."

"Fuck off then," she says lightly.

"I can't. A moth to a flame. I want you."

"So, what am I supposed to do?" asks Maggie. They walk on in silence. Then Maggie says, "You know, Martin, you don't really like me, either."

Martin is stunned. In his heart he believes what she has just said, but still he is busily rejecting it. *"I love this women. Well, fuck it, anyway: I want this women."*

NINE

It's evening of Martin's Ticket Collector encounter. He opens the door to the long hallway of his Palmeira Square apartment. Amy is coming down the hall to greet him cheerfully.

"Hello. You're late."

"Yep. I got lost again."

Amy embraces and kisses Martin. She is in apparently great spirits. "Dinner's ready, and not yet cold. Cheese flan, onions and hiziki, and avocado salad." They start back up the hall. "Guess who phoned."

Martin stops and puts his hand to his heart. "Oh... Was she drunk?"

"I couldn't tell. The phone had hiccups."

"What did she want?"

"Oh, just to chat... 'How are you.' She's lonely."

"What did you chat about?"

"Oh, this and that. Of course I mentioned that you'd strained your shoulder and so couldn't write your thesis at the moment, but I..."

"I asked you not to tell her anything about me!"

"Martin. I was joking. What's wrong with you?"

"I don't know."

"She can't hurt you."

"I don't know."

Martin and Amy sit at the kitchen table. Martin sits listlessly kneading his shoulder. He has hardly touched his food. Now he perks up. "I'm still the master of fate," he says. "I'm just taking a few days off." He ponders. Wrinkles his brow. "Why don't you go out? Go see that film you wanted us to go to. My horoscope says I'll be excellent company next week. Hold on." Martin sinks again into his despondency. He plays absently with his food.

Amy reaches breaking point. She drops her cutlery onto her plate. "I can't bear it anymore. I can't bear it." She gets up, agitatedly. "Yes! I'm going out!" She walks huffily down the hall. Martin just sits there. The front door slams. Martin closes his eyes. Eyes closed, he sees the ever closing door. This time it is Amy who is swinging it closed.

TEN

St. Anne's Well Gardens, a park in Brighton, a sunny morning. Martin walks through the playground. He is relaxed, even happy. He is carrying a shopping bag which he holds now to his chest. He passes a mother pulling her child along by the arm out of the sand-pit. The mother's voice is strident. "You do as I say!" she shouts. The child is crying. But there are happier children in the park too, on swings, on slides, on the roundabout.

Martin walks on.

Maggie's room is in morning disarray when the doorbell rings. She gets out of bed dressed in tee-shirt and panties. She walks down the corridor to open the door to Martin. Meeting, they almost embrace, but she's too ambivalent, standoffish. Martin ends up pecking her on the cheek. The shopping bag hangs from his left hand. Maggie asks what's in it.

"Some goodies for the trip," Martin answers. "Are we tripping?" They start back down the corridor.

"We'll see how we feel," says Maggie. "Either way, I've got to clean the flat up first." The floor of Maggie's room, the sitting room, is littered with dirty mugs and cups, the table with assorted dishes. Maggie opens the curtains. "Could you take the crockery through to the kitchen while I get dressed?"

There is a tray on the table. Martin collects the crockery from the table and the floor as Maggie is takes off her tee-shirt and puts on her blouse. She doesn't wear a bra. Martin stops to watch. She keeps her back to him. Still facing away, she brushes her hair, and Martin continues his task.

Maggie joins Martin in tidying the room. She starts by setting things straight while Martin makes the bed. The stereo is playing the Beatles' 'Abbey Road'. "She came in through the bathroom window Protected by a silver spoon..." Martin picks up Maggie's tee-shirt off the bed he is making. He looks around to see that she is not watching and buries his face in the tee-shirt before tucking it under the pillow.

Cycling through the hundred inevitables, Jimy Hendrix sings "Foxy lady! I'm coming to get you!" as Martin finishes vacuuming. Maggie is in the kitchen washing the dishes. Martin walks through to the kitchen. He goes over to Maggie at the sink and embraces her from behind. For a moment she responds, bending her head back against him. Then she squirms free. She hands him the washing-up brush. "Here. You finish," she says. She goes to fetch the broom and starts sweeping the floor while Martin finishes the dishes.

The sitting room, Maggie's room, is neat and tidy. Maggie is putting on another record. Richie Havens. She drops the needle onto the last track with only a slight scratching. Martin grits his teeth as he comes in with a tray bearing a glass of water and two pills. He raises the tray towards Maggie; it's a gesture of invitation and inquiry.
    "Put it on the table," she says. Richie Havens sings, "Let the river rock you like a cradle. Climb to the tree tops, child, if you are able…" Maggie goes over to the mirror above the mantle. She picks up some mascara and starts making up her eyes. Meanwhile Martin puts the tray down on the table and goes to sit on the bed watching Maggie raptly.
    Maggie, finishing, turns her attention to Martin. Through the mirror she watches him watching her. "Don't look at me like that!"
    Martin turns away, hunching up his nagging shoulder even further. But almost instantly he gets up and starts pacing. He starts to talk in a perturbed manner, without looking at Maggie. "That I can't stand. That prohibition." He addresses Maggie directly. "My mother used to flaunt herself in front of me with that prohibition: 'don't look at me'."
    "You're staring, you're staring, you're staring at me. What do you want from me?"
    "Maggie. I was only looking at you. Savouring you."

"Did you savour your mother?"

"No, good God. Not savour. Let God save her."

"Don't talk like that!... Do I remind you of her?"

"Yes, and of my father, and you often look just like my sister. Most of all you remind me of me... That's your attachment to me too, isn't it? You see yourself in me."

"I didn't know I had any attachment."

"So," says Martin, "I'm hoping I'll be able to work out all my family involvements through you. You're the whole world to me."

Maggie walks over to the table. She takes a tablet from the tray, and the glass. She holds up the glass to toast. "To the whole world," she says. She puts the pill in her mouth, drinks, and swallows. Maggie's decision, and action, is abrupt, but Martin too takes his tab and the glass and toasts, "To light, life and love."

"Shhh!" Maggie cautions. "Desire is the devil's whip."

They sit down on the floor opposite one another. Maggie lights a stick of incense and holds it staring into the smoke. Richie Havens is singing, "...don't mind me cause I ain't nothing but a dream." Martin is observing himself. Defining himself. He feels that he is distracted, and he feels that he is very focused. Too focused. He watches Maggie and the incense smoke rising round her. Martin judges that he is very ambivalent yet closed minded. Martin's mind is so busy, so restless. He recites one of his poems to himself silently in his head, perhaps to silence the voices:

"Sister! Black sister, ride forth. I am your chariot. I kiss your spur, and it, and it, I kiss the Gorgon's lair. I have followed to your deep realm, where I stroked and poked you, where I stoked you, or is that too much? Just what is 'love'?"

Time flows. The music needs changing. Martin puts on the Rolling Stones, 'Aftermath', "Going Home". He's putting the Cream's 'Goodbye' album back into its sleeve and into its jacket. He kneels to do this beneath a poster of Indian deities coupling. He looks up at Maggie. "How long has it been."

"I don't know," she says. "Maybe an hour."

"Are you getting anything off the acid?"

"Nope. Not even a paisley. What did you pay for the stuff?'

"A pound a hit."

"Sucker."

Martin comes over and sits cross legged across from Maggie. They sit a while without speaking. Maggie asks the classic Zen Koan, "What is the sound of one hand clapping?" She extends her arm and very slowly swings it round, slowly swings stopping an inch from Martin's ear. She has his rapt attention. She rolls backwards, somersaults away from him, to end up kneeling. She shifts to recline on her elbow and asks quietly, "Daddy, where is here?"

Martin, lost in the dust motes, is suspended between the rush of his restless mind and... epiphany.

Maggie has put on some Indian music. The tabla is dancing. Martin has set out a bottle of wine and some wine glasses. He pulls from the carrier bag, like a rabbit from a hat, and arranges on a plate on the floor where Maggie is sitting, "Bagels... cream cheese... a taste, just a taste, of smoked salmon... cheese cake, the food kind... and a pineapple."

"Beautiful," says Maggie, slicing and spreading the bagels, while Martin opens the wine. "How's Amy?" she asks.

"Oh, well enough. Still very efficient at everything. Still shy and insecure. Still very loyal. Still teaching school..." Martin pops the cork on the bottle and tells Maggie, as he starts to pore the wine, that he thinks that Amy is a bored with her job.

"What Amy needs," says Maggie, "is a man."

"Thank you," says Martin.

"A devoted man. Someone who gives a damn about her."

"I'll give her your message," says Martin.

They clink their glasses together.

The stereo plays Country Joe and the Fish's 'Electric Music...' - stoned mood music. "Hey, Partner, won't you pass that reefer round. My head is spinning, yeah, can't seem to touch the ground..." Martin feels far too sober. The floor is scattered with empty plates. Martin and Maggie sit on the floor in distant poses. Martin is staring out the window as he asks Maggie, "Are you getting anything from the acid?" Outside the window of the basement apartment there are trees, the bass of trees near by, the middles and tops of trees beyond. And there are birds singing.

"No," Maggie answers. "Not a whisper. And you?"

"No," says Martin. "We should've stuck to deep breathing. You don't get as high, but it's cheaper and much more reliable." He passes a "joint" to Maggie. It's an "English joint", tobacco and hash, three papers. Etiquette has one sitting with it a while and puffing leisurely on it several times before passing it. "Still," he says, "this is a pleasant enough way to spend the afternoon."

The afternoon sun comes into the room. Dust motes again. The music is the Grateful Dead's "Come hear Uncle John's band playing to the tide..." Maggie and Martin are rolling on the floor together, giggling. They end up with Maggie kneeling over Martin, legs astride him, one arm either side on his head, her long dark hair hanging down around his head. He looks up through the cavern of her hair into her shadowed face. *"This is a moment I will remember,"* he thinks. She is smiling.

Jenny and her boy friend, John, enter the room. "Oh, I hope I'm not interrupting anything," she says.

Maggie and Martin disengage. "No," says Martin. "Not at all. Come and join us." He's joking.

"Later, Maybe," she replies. "Cup of tea?"

Maggie, Jenny and John huddle close together, téte a téte, each with a steaming tea mug. John is Jenny's boyfriend, twenty year old, a freshman and a hippy. A hippy like a fish in water. The three freshmen sit almost head to head. The conversation is inconsequential. The music is Crosby Stills Nash and Young's 'Deja Vu', "And I feel like I've been here before..."

"…so he said he might drop by tonight with an ounce for us…" says Jenny.

"What is it?" John interrupts.

"Oh, black Pak, I think. Anyway, I've no idea whether in the event we'll be so honoured…"

"Well, at least he pays his way…" says Maggie.

"… cause I told him not to bother…' Jenny continues.

"You what!?" says John.

Martin sits alone at the table with his tea anxiously tapping his fingers to the music. He is bored. Jenny continues: "…or at least, I told him not to put himself to any bother. He may bring the dope, but all he's gonna do is sit round the walls and drool."

"Oh, Jenny," says Maggie, "I hope you haven't been too cruel."

"You can talk!" Jenny quips back.

The album has changed It's the Jefferson Airplanes 'After Bathing at Baxter's Beach'; "Saturday Afternoon", a smoky haze. Dusk is falling. Maggie closes the curtains. Annie talks to Peter. They've just arrived. Jenny is sitting on John's lap in the armchair. They relate to each other with laughter.

Martin sits alone. He's smoking, toking. John reaches towards him. "Don't Bogart that joint."

And the Doors are playing 'Strange Days', "When the music's over…" The room is getting quite crowded. In addition to Maggie, Martin, Jenny, John, Peter and Annie, there is Matthew Luke and Mark, and a Mary. Luke is rolling a joint. Annie, Peter and Matthew are huddled talking. Maggie is dancing.
Round the walls sit Jenny and John, tête a tête, and Mark, Mary, and Martin. Several joints are being smoked and passed around. The music is loud.

Maggie stops dancing and goes over to speak with Annie. Annie nods an affirmation. Maggie comes over to Martin, kneels and leans forward to speak into his ear above the music. "I've got a headache, and I think I'm coming down with a cold. I'm going through to Anne's room."

"Me too!" says Martin.

He follows her down the hall, to Anne's room. Then sits in the armchair smiling.

Maggie closes the curtains and lights a candle. "What are you so happy about?"

"Nothing, nothing. Why are you so glum?"

"I've got a splitting headache, for God's sake!" She frowns as she goes over to switch on the lamp by the bed. A thin shawl has been thrown over the shade, veiling it. The light is dim, warm. Maggie starts to undress. She peals off her tee-shirt - she wears no bra. Her bosom is petite. She shrugs out of her tight jeans. Not much waist or hips. A boy's body. She slips off her panties and sock, and gets into bed.

Martin comes over to the bed. "Move over," he says.

"Oh no you don't, Martin. There is no way that you are getting into this bed with me."

"I was only going to sit by you. I was going to offer to massage your head and neck."

Says Maggie, coyly, but archly, "Oh, neck is it." She moves over to make room for Martin to sit. He reaches out to massage her brow, but she forestalls him with a sharp, "No, don't touch me!"

Martin lies down on top of the covers. He stares at the ceiling. "Oh, Mag, I want so much to know you, to comfort you, to feel you, to touch you. Tell me 'maybe'."

"Maybe."

"I really want to trip with you. It means a lot to me."

"We tried."

"I wonder if... Do you think..."

"I don't think anything. I don't feel anything. I don't know anything. I don't see anything. I don't hear anything. I have no opinions, no dreams, no plans. I don't remember anything, and I don't wish to anticipate anything. There is nothing here for you to query."

"Oh, Maggie, Maggie, I love you."

"Have you ever had some little moon-eyed girl following you round, desperate for you to ball her, dogging you everywhere you go? Making you feel like a heel every time you turn away? It's a bore."

"Yes, I know. I can't help myself."

"Martin, you can't always have what you want."

"Oh, Maggie, Maggie. If I can't have you, I wish you didn't exist. Ohhh, I wish you were dead."

"Charming," says Maggie.

Martin, behind his eyes, watches his ever-closing door slam shut.

ELEVEN

Martin and Amy's sitting room doubles as his study. Martin is sitting at his desk working on his thesis. He writes longhand. He writes, stops to think, writes again, stops, writes... Then he crumples up the paper and throws it at the bin. The bin by now is overflowing in a great mound of crumpled paper. Martin looks at the mound, huffs at the cliché of it. Then he leans forward to rest his face in his hands. *"If I sit here long enough something's bound to come,"* he thinks. He can hear his heart beating. He listens. He's been acutely aware of his heart beat for a few days now. Hitherto he has heard his heart beat, as it were, "internally", inside himself. Now he hears it "externally", outside of himself, "thup..thup..thup.." He hears not the "heartbeat" itself, but the heart beating against the chest wall. The sound seems to actually emanate from his chest wall.

Martin gets up. The sound fades. Martin listens, puzzled. He wonders what to do. He leaves the room, walks up the hall to the phone which is off the hook. He picks up the receiver, pushes the "button" to get a dial tone, starts to dial, but stops, biting his lip. He puts down the receiver, again off the hook.

Martin goes back to the sitting room and reclines on the sofa to read. His back rests against the arm of the sofa so that his chest is again hunched forward. The ominous sound returns. "Thup..thup..thup.."

Martin looks up as he hears the sound of the front door opening and closing. "That you, Amy?"

"Hello," she calls.

Martin calls back. "Could you put the phone back on the hook?"

Moments later Amy enters the room. She's in her work clothes. She looks very school-marmish in a short-skirt, with her hair tied up, carrying a stack of exercise books. "How fared the day?" Martin asks.

"Oh, so so. Biology with 4A is impossible. All they want to do is look inside my nickers. And you?"

Amy passes near to Martin who reaches his hand up under her skirt. "Oh, yes, me too, every time," he says.

Amy slips away from him. "No, silly. How did your day go?"

"Well… Now don't get frightened…"

"That's put the fear of God in me for starters." For a moment Amy looks apprehensive. Then she asks, "What's happened? Did your mother call?"

"Something's wrong with my heart."

"That, I know."

"No, really. I don't know what it's about, but I can hear my heartbeat externally. Maybe it's some sort of message."

"Hmm," says Amy.

"It's not a joke. Really, I can hear it. Not inside my head or chest, but sort of here..." Martin gestures, cupping both hands round the space just before his chest. "…outside. Here, see if you can hear it."

Amy comes over and sits on the edge of the sofa where Martin is reclining. She bends her head down to his chest. "No," says Martin, "try and see if you can hear it from about a foot away, first."

Amy holds her head 8 or 10 inches away from Martin's chest. Thup..thup..thup. "Yes!" exclaims Amy. "Amazing. I wonder what it could be?"

"It's my heart, obviously, but what does it mean? I think the heart must be beating against the chest wall. But why? It could be anything. Whatever it is, it's frightening."

"Yes," say Amy. "Cup of tea and dinner. What else should we do?"

"Take two aspirin, and doctor in the morning."

"Right," says Amy. "Doctor in the morning."

Martin and Amy are having coffee after dinner in the kitchen by candle light. Amy has changes into more elegant clothes, a long skirt, her hair brushed out free. Martin stubs out his cigarette, takes a sip of coffee, and lights up another fag.

"I don't think you should smoke so much," says Amy.

"Don't worry. I'm not doing any dope until I've sorted out this heart thing. But I don't think smoke has anything to do with it."

"I meant cigarettes."

"In that case, I'll do my best." Martin stubs out the newly lit cigarette. He frowns. "You think I'm smoking too much dope? I am getting the thesis done."

"Well, things seem to be getting on top of you." Amy pauses. "You'll see the doctor again tomorrow about your heart, yes?"

"Yes, I will," says Martin, irritated. "Of course. But I won't get any light out of Griffin. He doesn't like discussing symptoms."

"Well, you go along and be nice and polite, and maybe for a change he'll tell you what's wrong with you."

Martin gets up and starts to clear the table. "I doubt it. He's too much the amateur psychologist. Like your 4A, he only wants to crawl into ones sex-life. Antibiotics or the couch. That's all the Student Centre doctors seem to know of." Martin, as he walks to the sink laden with dishes, sallies on in a loud voice, "Oh, yes, and tranqs. Fill our cranks full of tranqs till they fill up the tanks, then juggle their sensibilities with a jolt of 'lectricity, and if all else fails, why, lob off a lobe or two... loboo loboo bottomy..." Martin returns to wipe down the table. "Anyway, there's one redeeming side to all this."

"Mmmm," Amy hums as Martin sits down again.

"I've been reading these three apparently very different philosophies: Alan Watts' "the way of Zen"; Christ, Matthew's Gospel; and Norman O. Brown's very fine reinterpretation of Freud, "Life Against Death". You should read it." Amy frowns at this, as Martin continues, "And they all connect together. They're all preaching that there is only the eternal Now, and that Now is
eternal." Martin stares into the candle flame. "And repression, fear and anxiety, darken one's light. So one has to try to be as aware and awake as possible. There's nothing else. Reflect everything, like a mirror. Being here and now, and being spontaneous..." Martin gets up and starts wiping down the table again. "...and that way we can avoid Ego and premeditation and living before and after the event. And now I find that it's a very practical philosophy. I can work it. 'Sufficient to the day is the evil thereof.' I'm not the least bit frightened... touch wood." Martin lifts the corner of the table cloth to "touch wood". In doing so he overturns and spills the milk jug. He and Amy grab at the jug. Martin rights it with his right hand. He shrugs, but his mouth is clenched in an expression of grim resignation.

Martin is reading in bed. Amy is asleep. The sound of Martin's heart beating against his chest wall continues incessantly, "Thup..thup..thup". Martin puts down the book, switched off the light. He lies down, pulling the covers up to his neck. A street light plays through the curtains onto his face. Martin lies there thinking. "So *far so good. I'm doing alright. Here I am with days, or weeks, or years left to live, and I'm not the least bit frightened."* Then the thought occur to him, and he thinks, *"What if I do panic?"* With this the "thupping" gets louder and louder and faster. Martin becomes very tense. *"Oh, my God!"* He starts to vibrate and then quite literally to bounce on the bed with every heart beat. He calls out. "Amy!"

Amy wakes. "What's wrong? What's the matter?"

"I... I was thinking... how well I was doing... and then... I panicked."

Amy switches on the light. "What do you want me to do?"

"Phone the doctor."

Amy looks at her watch. "It's two o'clock in the morning."

"Phone the doctor!"

"Alright. Hold on."

Amy gets up. She wears a nighty, and puts on a dressing gown. Meanwhile Martin continues to literally bounce on the bed.

Amy returns from the phone in the hallway. Martin is still in a panic, though it is no longer at its peak. His body jerks spasmodically with his heart beat. "What, what took so long," he asks.

"I had to phone Dr. Hertz. It's not Griffin's turn to make night calls."

"But Griffin... only lives round the corner..."

"And Hertz lives ten miles away..."

"Oh God..."

"He'll be about twenty minutes. He said just try to relax... Would you like a cup of tea, or something?"

Martin holds out a shaking hand to Amy. "Just hold my hand."

Amy comes over and sits on the bed holding Martins hand and stroking his forehead.

Dr. Hertz arrives without a smile. Dr. Hertz is a young late thirties, tall and insensitive. He examines Martin, listening to his chest with a stethoscope. Martin tries to explain to himself. "I was thinking what would happen if I panicked, and I panicked."

"Well, you seem calm enough now. You're perfectly fit, young man. What you've just suffered is a panic attack. It is simply fear and adrenalin. It's really just a bout of tachycardia, that's all. The heart races. It runs its course in about ten or fifteen minutes. It can be very frightening, but there's nothing to worry about." Dr. Hertz rummages through his bag, produces and assembles a syringe. "I'll give you a mild sedative so that you can sleep tonight...' He injects Martin in the biceps. He moves hastily and without care, and it's painful. Martin flinches and mouths an agonized "Oh". Dr. Hertz continues, "...and if you'll call in to see Dr. Griffin in the morning you can discuss the matter more fully with him then, and I can get back to Kingston and perhaps get a little sleep myself."

"But why," Martin asks, "am I hearing my heart beat externally? Why is it beating against the chest wall? What's displacing it?"

Amy enters the bedroom with a tray bearing a pot of tea, cups, milk, sugar, as Dr. Hertz answers. "Anatomically speaking, the heart does not beat against the thoracic wall. Sensitive people, hypersensitive people are often conscious of their heart beating inside their chest, and project this, so that you think you hear your heart externally. That's what you've done. It's a trick the mind likes to play."

Martin protests, "But Amy heard it too!"

Hertz glances at Amy, and then back. "Young man, in fifteen years of medical practice I have never come across this "symptom" you describe, nor have I ever come across any mention of it in any medical literature..."

"But Amy..."

Hertz is packing up his bag and preparing to leave. "If you'll excuse me, I have a long drive ahead of me. Don't forget to make an appointment to see Dr. Griffin tomorrow." He moves over to the door. "Goodnight," he says curtly. Amy comes over to the bedroom door as Dr. Hertz exits with an, "I'll see myself out, thank you."

Martin shouts after him, "Thanks for allaying my fears! Very comforting"

Amy pours the tea, two cups. The third cup's left empty. Martin complains, "My God, doctors! The stupid, arrogant... I'll get no joy from Griffin tomorrow, I know. I'll ring up and make an appointment with Dr. Wright, the head of the practice. I think he's more down to earth. He might be prepared to discuss the symptoms. After all, he is an old family friend, and one of father's students."

And meanwhile Martin's heart is calling softly, "thup..thup.."

TWELVE

Mid-morning next day Martin enters the campus Student Health Centre, Drs.Wright, Griffin and Hertz' "surgery". He goes over to the receptionist. "I'm Martin Howard. I have an appointment to see Dr. Wright at ten thirty."

"One moment. Let me see." She looks at the appointment book. "Ah! Mr. Howard. You are one of Dr. Griffin's patients, are you not?"

"Yes, but I have an appointment with..."

"In that case you will have to see Dr. Griffin."

"I'm happy too see Dr. Griffin anytime. He's a very pleasant man and I'm very fond of him, but right now I have an appointment with Dr. Wright."

"Dr. Griffin will see you now."

"Well... alright. I'll see Dr. Griffin first so long as I get to keep my appointment with Dr. Wright afterwards."

"You will have to consult with Dr. Griffin."

"Do I or don't I get to see Dr. Wright?"

"You will have to ask Dr. Griffin about your concern..."

"Oh! You silly old zombie! I hope you strangle in your red tape."

Martin rushes out, slamming the door.

Martin has spent the day frantically trying to find a doctor, find out about his symptoms. The library didn't help. Now he's pacing the kitchen. Amy is serving tea and trying to be sympathetic. Martin has set up an appointment, for the next day, to see her doctor.

"Dr. Goodwin?" Amy asks.

"No. Dr. MacEwin. I guess he's a partner." Martin ruminates, "Maybe I don't need a medical opinion to clarify my heart. Maybe I need to see a spiritualist to clarify the message? Maybe I need a priest? Christ! My realities are falling to pieces."

"Maybe you should see your father? After all, he is a chest specialist."

"No! All I need now is a lecture on my filial duties. That's what I'd get from Professor Martin Howard. 'It wouldn't hurt you to look after your mother.' That, of course, is called passing the buck. Or is it passing the doe?"

The telephone rings. Martin is startled. Amy looks at him with a hard face. She is getting fed up with his weakness and fear. She gives a huffy sigh and turns to go answer the phone.

Martin sits with his tea. Amy returns. She is hard, cold, cut-off. "Your mother. Confirming the arrangements for the Swedish bazaar."

"I wish you wouldn't see her."

"What are you going to do when we have children? Will they never see their Granny?" Now Amy softens somewhat. "Martin. Are you at all interested in having children? I'm not getting any younger."

"Amy, Amy, I don't feel ready yet, Amyamy..." These last words, which fade away, are mumbled and slurred so that they come out somewhat like "Mummy". Martin continues abstractly. "I just want to know if I'm dying or not. I mean, if

I'm going to die in a year or so, I don't want to spend my last few months on my bloody thesis. I'm probably alright, but I just want to know... I hope I don't panic again." During this monologue Amy gets up and starts tidying the kitchen. She cannot get into his philosophications, his verbal dribble. He rambles on, "Do you remember in Huxley's 'Island' where the old woman is dying. She takes some mushroom and trips out alert and clear as a bell. Huxley did that himself. He was dying of cancer and the morning came he knew he was going to die: he dropped two hundred and fifty micrograms and went out crystal clear, grokking it all...""

For Amy, Martin's voice, and Martin, are fading away.

Goodwin and MacEwin's surgery is in a high rise on Hove Boulevard. Dr. MacEwin's office is large and plush. Dr. MacEwin sits behind his large cherry wood desk. He is in his mid-sixties, rather round, with small lensed glasses. He affects a Viennese manner and accent, though he is, in fact, Scottish.

Martin sits in an armchair on the other side of the desk. The seating is arranged so that Martin has to look up to the doctor. Martin is has just started telling his story. "...So, I need information about this symptom. I don't think there's any point in my wasting your time going into why I've come to you, rather than my own doctor, but I can't get any information out of him..."

"I know, I know," says MacEwin solicitously (in his Viennese accent). "You are too big for them," (pronounced 'zem').

Martin is surprised by this seemingly irrelevant comment, but he ignores it and goes straight on. "You see, I strained my shoulder and since then my heart has felt as if it were beating against my chest, and I can hear it..."

"Vell now," say MacEwin, "let us see vot ve can do vor you. Are you veeling relaxed and comvortable now?"

"Yes, thank you."

"Good... Now, dzell me, do you have any phobias"

"Yes," says Martin.

"Don't be afraid. Yust relax... Vot are zese phobias?"

Martin's good at this game - he is into psychology - and he answers quickly off the top of his head, "Heights, fish, my mother's fanny."

MacEwin, not having listened to Martin's answer, almost interrupts him to ask, "Dell me, do you ever get a jooting pain up your anus?" With this MacEwin holds out his hand with the middle finger extended upwards, and thrusts it vigorously upwards.

"No," Martin answers, a little bit shocked. "Tell me, doctor, what are your phobias?"

"I am ze doctor. I ask ze questions."

"Yes, but what are your phobias?"

The doctor becomes tense. He begins to raise his voice (and loses most of his Viennese accent). "I am the doctor! I ask the questions!"

Martin, with a mocking face, raises his hand like a school child asking permission to speak. Dr. MacEwin, losing control, rises to his feet, waving his hands about. "You, you get out. Get out of my office. Out, out, out!"

Martin, too, rises. "Zank you, doctor. Good dzay."

Martin and Amy sit in the living room on the sofa. Martin has been recounting his interview with MacEwin. Amy is in hysterics, laughing. "I don't believe it," she splutters.

"It's true. Every vord. Cross my heart and hope to die." He crosses his heart, and asks, "Have you ever see the man?"

"No. I've always seen the younger one, Dr. Goodwin. He's quite reasonable, if a bit... gushy... unctuous, that's the word: and he's drawn to the 4A complex."

"4A complex?"

"The answer's in the nicker, silly... Cup of tea?"

"Yes, that would be nice. Everything's alright as long as there's a nice hot cup of tea. One of the two universal panaceas, tea is."

"And the other?"

"Ask 4A," says Martin.

Amy smiles. She gets up and goes to the door where she stops and turns back to Martin. "You'll <u>have</u> to go to your father, won't you?"

Martin looks up at the ceiling as if he hadn't heard. Then, lowering his head, but still not looking at Amy, he answers, "Yes," in the manner of a sigh.

THIRTEEN

Prof. Howard, having just examined Martin, crosses to his desk. He takes his stethoscope from round his neck, puts it away in it's case, and puts the case away in his desk. During these maneuvers, and subsequently, Prof. Howard speaks to, but does not often look directly at, Martin. Meanwhile, Martin puts his shirt and jacket back on, and asks, "So, what's the diagnosis?"

"I hope it doesn't disappoint you too much, but I don't think there's anything seriously wrong. I'd hazard that the trouble is largely psychosomatic, and about such matters I don't feel qualified to speak."

Martin comes over and sits in the chair on the other side of the desk from his father. "But what about my hearing the heartbeat externally. Amy heard it too!"

"I don't doubt it. I personally have never come upon this phenomenon, but several of my patients have described it to me. It doesn't seem to be indicative, diagnostically, of any one thing in particular. There's nothing seriously wrong with you organically. As to what precisely is going on, well, you're the psychologist."

"How come nobody else seems to have heard of this?"

"It's not in the medical textbooks."

"But you've heard of it."

"Yes, but then I make a habit of listening to what my patients have to say." Martin places his elbows on the desk and cover his face with his hands as his father continues. "If you feel you need to talk about things to someone… If you want to undertake some psychotherapy, I can finance it…" Martin lifts his head a bit, and brings his hands together, so that the index fingers hold his nose. He stares coldly at his father, who asks, "What's the matter?"

Martin, making his right hand into a fist, cupped in his left hand, and rests his chin on the left hand, his elbows still on the desk. "I was just thinking about what you were saying."

"About the therapy?"

"No."

There is a short pause and then Prof. Howard speaks, slightly flustered. "But I do… I do listen to what my patients say." The Professor gets up and starts to pace. He turns to Martin. "There's another matter, Martin. Why haven't you phoned your mother?"

Martin does not answer. The Professor presses on. "She keeps phoning me. To ask about you! I don't want to speak to her! She called me every night this week! I can't take any more of it! She's your mother! It's driving me crazy! You phone her!"

FOURTEEN

Martin and Amy sit together talking on the sofa. Martin is telling of his visit with his father. "…And he doesn't thinks it's necessarily something to get alarmed over. That's the most of it, and it's an immense relief. I was vanishing for a while there, I can tell you. Now maybe I can puzzle out what's really going on: why my heart, my real, honest to goodness, pumping heart is beating against my real honest to goodness chest, thup, thup, thup. Oh, and he said, when I pressed him, that it would be cool for me to drink or smoke in moderation. Admitted that it might help relax me."

"Well, that's a great relief," says Amy.

"Yeah… I think I will go and have a drink and a smoke and a think about it all."

Martin is in the bedroom kneeling, sitting on his ankles in front of the wardrobe mirror. There is an empty glass beside him. He is smoking a "joint". His shoulders are characteristically very hunched, and his heart is speaking, whispering out from his chest, "thup.. thup.. thup". Martin studies himself in the mirror. He puts his right hand to his left pectoralis, his chest, and eases his shoulder back. As he straightens the "thupping" fades and stops! He straightens his back and shoulder. Light seems to gather in his sight, his field of vision, round his mirror image face, as enlightenment dawns. He jumps up. "I've got it!" He hurries into the living room, elated, to explain excitedly to Amy, "I've figured it out. It starts with the seance, that "drop dead" message; Maggie wishing me dead, and me wanting to withdraw and cosset myself. Lots of death wishes flashing around that evening; and the shoulder strain. That's the physical hinge and vehicle of the drama. The conspiring event. See, with the shoulder pain I drop my shoulder…" which he now does, "and that puts me into the attitude and posture of fear. Being in the posture of fear tends to accentuate the anxiety, and to lock me in those anxious spaces, right, and that only tends to accentuate the slooping posture." Martin holds his pectoral muscle again, and straightens. "Now, the pectoral muscle, which helps brace and pull the shoulder, attaches on the breast." He flexes the shoulder and chest. "The pectorals tend to brace and raise the chest itself, and when you shloop your shoulder forward and down, collapse your chest… See? And when I was also bending forward, like when I was hunched up reading on the sofa, collapsing my chest even further, my heart actually did beat against my chest, thup, thup, making all those little shlurpy spaces round the edge, hlurp, hlup: got it Amy? Shllurp, shllurp." With his face he invites and coaxes Amy to "shlurp" along with him.

"Shllurp, shllurp," says Amy joining in with a comic, beaming face as Martin concludes, "And there, that's my heart symptom. When I straighten my shoulder the symptom disappears,"

Martin goes over to the window and looks out on the square. He sees the cut logs in he distance. "The logs! I can collect that beautiful piece of wood now.

Martin hurries out. He doesn't stop and bother to put on a coat, but rushes over to the cut logs..

In his fantasies Martin is a lumberjack. He is putting the finishing axe stroke onto a large tree, which starts to fall. He calls out, like his fantasy lumberjack calling *"Timber!"*, he calls out into the cold air of Palmiera Square, "Death and castration!" To himself he says, *"I fell and dismember..."* He has a memory of the park keepers buzz-sawing the felled elm into logs. This image folds into an image of himself, Martin, dragging an Christmas tree home through the snow. His internal monologue, accompanying these images, identify the image as... *"I fell and dismember the father's phallus."* His imaginings continue with a memory of a large, public-square with a tall decorated Christmas tree and with people gathered round, and nativity figures, and carol singing, while he finishes his monologue telling himself that he is "Preserving and celebrating round it," (it: "the father's phallus"?) "celebrating, round it, my birth." (Martin is a psychologist, practiced in psychobabble.)

Looking down at the logs, at his feet, Martin notices that there is a crocus blooming (unseasonably) next to the cut log he covets. Green leaves and purple flower, yellow stamen. Martin smiles at the flower as he stoops to pick up the log, and hoists it on to his left shoulder.

Martin comes back to the flat, carrying the log into the sitting room. He stands it by the hearth. He hies to the bedroom and returns with some of Amy's necklaces, which he festoons on the log. He turns around to hunt for some incense and sticks it the bark, lodges it there and lights it. He places a candle by the log, and lights that in turn.

Amy, who is correcting homework, looks up and watches all this bemused. "What is it?" she asks.

"A token," says Martin. "A totem absurdity." He bows down before his totem, head to the ground.

Amy comes over, kneels down, takes a brooch from her blouse, and pins it into the log. She too bows before the totem. They are enjoying themselves. Martin sits up, and looking at Amy, says, ""Perhaps it will sprout?"

They go over and sit together on the sofa. "Ah, I feel much better," says Martin. "And I feel much closer to you. Things are much better between us."

"Yes, you've felt you've needed me these last few days."

Martin ponders, "Mmmm?"

"And what about Maggie?" Amy asks.

"That's over now. I've worked that one through. Thank you for your patience. Let's go out together tomorrow night. Let's go dancing."

"What about tonight?"

"No. I'm tired. Exhausted."

"I'm going to the Swedish bazaar with your mother tomorrow."

"Oh... Well, what about Sunday, then?" asks Martin. "We can go out to the country."

Amy responds hesitantly. "I though you were seeing Maggie Sunday."

"What gave you that idea?"

"Well, you said something a while back about going up to London to some Rock concert."

"Ah, Amy, I'd have told you if I was going. Anyway, it's you I want to be with, little lady."

Amy gets up, goes over to the mantle piece, touches something on it. She turns round. "Umm... Well, umm... actually... I've arranged to go out sailing with Peter, and, mmm, we're having dinner at his place afterwards."

Martin holds a stunned silence. Then he hums to himself, "Mmmm! Peter?" he queries. "Couldn't you break the arrangement?"

Amy straightens. "I'm not sure I want to."

There's another silence. After a moment Amy turns and leaves the room. Martin goes over to his desk, fiddles with his books and papers, and then just sits there. *"Everything's going to be alright,"* he tells himself. He starts rocking himself gently in his chair. *"There's no mystery. There's always an answer."*

The telephone starts ringing. Amy calls out from the bedroom, "I'm not answering it!"

The phone goes on ringing. *"I just have to straighten my shoulders,"* thinks Martin. The telephone rings on, while Martin tells himself, with no surprise, *"I can't feel my heart anymore."*

RIME, THE SNOWBOW, AND CHRISTMAS LIGHTS AT TI SHERIFF

There was something new this morning I'd not caught before. The sun through the frosted window sparkled with hints of colour almost there: reds, and blues, and green shards, specks. And I couldn't really tell if they were points of prism bright hues or washed out like the stars, red like Mars, and wiki tells me Rigel 's blue, as are "the brighter Pleiades".

I judge myself that it didn't hold my attention very long except to suggest I should try to write… What's a blue star, I wondered, and by the time I was back from the web with Rigel, the colours were gone (and the song, and the song). Just white and yellows left.

Course the lights were a little like the snowbow that I found a dog's years back. In the newish snow in the low sun, there's an arc (at, what? a hundred and thirty degrees? who knows) where the snow sparkles blue, crimson, green, orange, bright, bright specks, flecks. Oh, I was so proud to find the snowbow.

And this minds me, some, of Ti Sheriff's Christmas lights.

I was hitching through Wales in the mid seventies exploring the rural counter culture with the yen to join it. We were open souls, relatively, and I had an address where I could stay ("crash" we'd say). Ti Sheriff, the Sheriff's cottage, was in the Brecon Beacons halfway up a "mountain", way above the road. Angela had come there from Hackney with her biker beau, Mel, hair to his waist (if not his toes), and Angie's eleven year old, Nick. Nick was a restless child (this was before Attention Deficit, I guess) and Christmas in the new house with the new father was near driving Nick wild. So on Xmas eve Angie gave Nick a hash brownie. Nick fell into a reverie staring at the Christmas tree. Time for bed said mum eventually. Oh, said Nick, I never knew there were so many colours in a Christmas light.

A NIGHT WITH THE KIDS

"What's the nicest thing you ever did?" Sangeeta asked me. I used to think the nicest thing I'd ever done was getting Antonio onto look at the airplane. When I was eighteen I worked for the summer in Italy as a tourist company's junior representative. A major part of my responsibilities was to ride to the airport in Naples to welcome the guests and disperse them along the Amalfi coast at their various hotels, and to collect them again at the end of their stay, to return them from Sorrento, Positano, and Amalfi to the airport. Our clients arrived and departed on the weekends, so the coach drivers worked, in the summer season, from Friday morning to Monday night in an all but non-stop shuttle. Tourists from England, Germany, Scandinavia... Ours were from England.

As you may imagine, the coach drivers might be quite exhausted by the second day of their long weekend. Now this was no problem on the hairpin cliff-face road above the Mediterranean Sea, Capri in the distance. No, the problem came when we hit the autostrada. Then the sleepy drivers would slip into reverie, and I'd listen for that subtle change in the engine's hum or roar that echoed the driver's drift into sleep. When I'd hear the engine relax I'd hurriedly offer, "Cigaretta?" That was my job, waking the driver.

One day one of the drivers brought his eleven-year-old son, Antonio, with him. The father would drive the long loop half a dozen, or a dozen times each weekend from Sorrento to the airport, yet Antonio had never seen an airplane up close. Just in the sky out over the Bay of Naples. Little toys with all those people from the buses. "Oh, it's bigger than a bus," said his father. "I'll show you."

We drove along the Amalfi coast at night, to Salerno and the autostrada, to Naples and the airport. We disgorged our busload of sun burnt families flying to Birmingham or to Manchester.

The we had too wait till all the passengers safely had embarked and departed. Time was crawling through this weary watch when suddenly it occurred to me that if I asked the Air Italia people I could probably get the kid, Antonio, a tour of the plane. So I asked, and yes, two Air Italia agents accompanied us, me and Antonio, onto the plane. Almost immediately the passengers arrived, and we were ushered through the cockpit and down the pilot's separate gangway.

As I say, for a long time, decades, I felt that this was the nicest thing I'd ever done, so this is the story I told in response to Sangeeta's question, and in response to this story Sangeeta told me about her night with the kid.

One day Geeta went out with a friend to a movie matinee. After the film, they went out for a coffee. Geeta's friend ordered a drink, a pink lady, even though she knew she shouldn't. So Sangeeta too had to cheat, had to be weak. She ordered a chocolate milkshake though sugar, dairy, and chocolate didn't agree with her, and often induced quite strong reactions. By the time Sangeeta reached home she was feeling a little high, spacey, and apprehensive.

Sangeeta rented a room in a family house from a couple who fought all the time. There were two children to the troubled marriage; Rick, four, and Brit, two.

Little Brit was daddy's darling. Chubby and angelic, she was emotionally substantial, her solid presence belying her age. As Sangeeta entered the house, Brit was sitting on the bottom step of the stairs leading up to Geeta's room as though waiting for her. Brit's arms were folded decidedly across her chest. The two-year-old dumpling sat below the closed trellised stair-gate, immovable.

"Can I get past?" Sangeeta asked. Brit shook her head "no".

Beyond them, the door to the basement was closed. The parents were off behind the closed door battling. The odd sharp word drifted up to the main floor. The two kids were left to sit it out, to weather the storm clouds.

"Do you want to come up to my room?" Sangeeta asked the kids. Brit nodded a cursory "yes". Sangeeta opened the stair-gate. Little Brit grabbed her hand and surged up the stairs. Rick, mournful, followed. Where Brit, daddy's favourite, glowed with self-assurance, Rick, mummy's pet, lacked luster. Mother enveloped him, but without substance. The world might any moment swallow mummy, and any wind might blow little Rick away. The corners of his mouth dragged towards the floor as he shuffled up the stairs behind the young woman and the toddler.

Was it the milkshake that had Sangeeta's head whirling? She talked to the kids as best she could as she tidied her room compulsively. She tried to be there for them, but her head was spinning, and things needed to be put in their place.

"God must have a sense of humour," she told me as she related this story. God is a new word in her vocabulary. She felt that the Hindu gods of her fathers' were a fiction, but I use the concept, "God", in such a loose and general way that Geeta has begun to concede such a benign and defuse Divine principle might indeed exist.

There in the room with the two kids, her head swimming, Sangeeta prayed for help, and questioned how someone so near the edge - and here come the voices again - how she could be of any use.

"Shall I read you a story?" she asked. "Yes," nodded Brit sagely. Rick's assent was a mere twitch.

They went down to the living room where the kids' books lived. Geeta picked up a book, plonked herself on the sofa, and read: Jack and the Beanstalk. But both kids were listless. As Sangeeta read on - fee, fie, foe, fum - Brit wandered over to an aquarium on the other side of the claustrophobic blue-walled room, pulled over a chair, climbed upon to it, and made to pour her milk into the water.

"Wait!" Geeta shouted. Brit hesitated. Geeta explained that the milk might kill the fish.

"I want to kill mummy's fish," said little Brit.

"Do you know what it means to die?" Geeta asked.

"That's when they lie at the bottom of the water on their

side," said Rick.

"They stop," said Brit. "They go away."

"When I was little," Geeta recalled and told them, "I poured ketchup into my mother's fish tank. She was so proud of her fish. And all the fish died. It made me feel very sad. I'd really like it if you didn't kill these little guys."

"Okay," said Brit. "Let me sit on you lap."

Brit and Sangeeta sat a while and talked. Then Sangeeta began to feel Rick's absence, and she had the intuition that she should find him fast. She put Brit down, and went out into the hall, over to the stairs. Rick was upstairs. He had climbed over the banister, and was hanging down into the stairwell from the banister.

"Oh, Rick, be careful. You'll fall."

"I want to fall. I want to kill myself."

Sangeeta climbed the stairs, talking to Rick the while. As she approached him, he let go. She reached and caught him. They tumbled together into a heap on the stairs. Rick huddled up close to her.

Geeta had on an old sloppy jumper. It was open, unbuttoned. Her hands had been too shaky since the milkshake to fumble with the buttons. Now in the aftermath of her fright with Rick's fall, she shivered. And the little four-year-old boy helped her button up her jumper.

Brit came and joined them. And they hugged together, all three, a long while. Then Sangeeta put the children to bed.

I glowed quietly as Sangeeta told me the story. It made me feel useful, though I was never there, and the encounter was far from a cure for Geeta. But we got to look into the aeroplane and we 're getting ready to fly home.

SUITS AND HIPPIES

We were talking, here at Millennia's end, about "hippie". We were reflecting on the Summer of Love and the Counter Culture, and Annie said, Annie asked, "Do you think that you flower children defined a generation?"

"Yes," I said. "But while we were defining the generation of sixties and the seventies, the suits were putting a lock on the eighties and the nineties." And that got me thinking about Suzy. Suzy Knell.

Suzy was a hippie. She wore long cotton prints, flowing skirt, flowery blouses. No bra, of course. She walked round campus accompanied by Space, her one-eyed Harlequin Great Dane. This was nineteen seventy. I was the long-haired post-doc on campus, so Suzy singled me out to supervise her self-directed project. It was on feminism (and this is before feminism, just before feminism, I think), and it was great, her project. A+. She was thorough, dedicated, and bright.

The year before, in 1969 Suzy had been studying liberal arts at "Oakland University" in Ann Arbor, Michigan. Oakland was a liberal, nay, a progressive school, by policy half black and half white. Suzy and her boy friend, Mark, were politically active, as were their best friends, a black couple, Cathy and Franklin. Franklin was involved, peripherally, with the Panthers. Oh, there was revolution in the corridors, and parties every evening. But everything came apart, one day, when Suzy was taken hostage… literally.

She was taken hostage, held at gun point by a black person, probably not a student, and probably a little demented. She was held at gun point one summers day on campus, by a road side. For two hours she talked to her assailant, human to human. After two hours the perpetrator's attention wandered and she threw him over the hood, the bonnet of a car parked where they were standing. He landed heavily, awkwardly on his back, was incapacitated and was taken away in an ambulance.

No happy ending here though. Franklin, the panther, started

putting Mark down as less than a man for failing to avenge Suzy, a revenge he couldn't very well execute as Suzy refused, just for that reason, to give anyone any information. Well, with the best of friendships coming apart in this unpleasant manner, Suzy decided she had had as much as she could take of macho America. She
decided to come up to a quieter Canada to finish her studies. And she bought herself a Great Dane, Space.

But what reminded me of Suzy Knell, when speaking of the suits taking advantage of our playing around in the sixties to buy up and corner the world, was an incident that happened in Canada that winter that I was supervising her project. Suzy was up just north of Toronto at a ski lodge. She was leaving, in the parking lot getting in to her beat up VW van. A young business man, getting out of his BMW, looked her and one-eyed Space up and down and said, "We'll win, you know. We are going to beat you." And that in our kinder, gentler Canada too.

Moral? I'm not sure. But they will be taking care of business, you can be sure. (Indeed they have.)

TIME TRAVEL

I don't know how to write this story. I don't know even if we'll be alive tomorrow. And if we live long enough for you to read this, then it's probably all bull. But this is what the Professor told me. And he is a super star. They say he's the next Einstein. So I'll just tell it as it comes, what the hell.

I bumped into Professor Norardny in a bar on Queen's Street this evening. A bit of a dive. Him in a back corner. Still wearing his hat, pulled down over his eyes. I'd have hardly noticed him if he hadn't cut such a sad figure, hardly recognized him if I hadn't seen him so often over the last few years. I've got the small office across from his suite of rooms in the Physic Building. "Professor," I said.

He slowly put down his glass, wanly looked up. "Professor yourself," he said.

"Why so glum?"

"Oh, just the end of the world," says he.

"May I sit?"

"Suit yourself."

I did.

I'd best tell you about Norardny, though there are few who don't know something about him by now. He published his Noetic theory last year, on-line. Turned mind and consciousness into mathematics, and then a month later his meta-noetics turned matter into a sort of mind stuff, just like the mystics always said, and it and just happened to reconcile relativity and quantum. A theory of everything, and no ones been able to tear it down. Then there's the icing. For starters it seems about to solve all our energy problems with cheep, save, clean cold fusion.

"So why aren't you on top of the world, after you've explained the world, and it's at your feet?"

"Because, my friend, it's all going to end."

"Well, I guess we knew that even before your noetics. All things are impermanent, the Buddha said."

Norardny now fiddled with the straw that came with his

drink, looking away from me, looking down, mumbling. "The effing Caliphate and the Chinese. They'll probably have at each other before this night over. Tonight, mate. Tonight. How's that for doomsdays prophesy. You'll know if I'm crazy, if not tonight, then by the end of the week."

"I'm lost," I said. "Start at the beginning."

"It's time travel," he said. "It's time travel, so we're all going to be dead."

"There's no time travel."

"Exactly!" he said, while I stared at him blankly. "Look," he said, "my theory allows for time to move both ways, and just as simply as it gave us cold fusion, it's a simple matter to push things either way through time and space."

"But for the paradoxes," I said.

"Oh, you'd get used to the paradoxes. Where do you think my noetics came from? When I had my theory halfway there, why there it was. I'd sent the answers back to me."

"I'm sorry. You'll have to explain."

"Okay. What I'm saying is that about the time I had half the picture, voila, there on my desk, a folder, scrawled large on the cover, in my hand, it said, "Here it is. Arthur Norardny. You're welcome." It was dated almost two years in the future. In fact, I just typed it out and sent it to myself a month back. You see, once you understand the noetics, time travel is a snap in theory, and not that hard in practice. Took a while to sort out the scaling, cause we're moving all the time, so you've got to get the knack of latching on to context: context glues you. It wasn't that difficult after all and I've been sending articles, things, to me for a year. I've been receiving things from the future for two years. You get used to it. Its a few months now I've been sending animals. Actually, one of the worrying things is that at the moment I don't actually have anything from the future."

He paused. Stared at his drink. I let a moment pass and then said clumsily, "You're kidding me."

"No," he half laughed. "Actually, it was a bit of a joke. First animals I sent were earthworms. Like Calvin."

"Calvin?"

"Calvin and Hobbes. Never mind. Anyway, I've sent mice. I've sent the cat. I had two copies of The Pookey for a year, and they weren't clones. Himself it was, and he didn't much like himself. I had to keep him apart."

"You're kidding."

"Not a bit of it,' said he. "Once you get used to, it's just the new norm. And that's the rub."

"The rub?"

"The problem. See, I've built the machine. The man size machine. The "Time Machine". And I've sent the cat back again with it. Yeah, for a week I had three Pookeys. And I'm ready to go myself, tomorrow even, or the next day. And you see, the problem is, once there's time travel, there will always have been time travel."

"Well, yes, I guess. But there isn't."

"Just so. In any civilization where they develop time travel, it will always have been. They will live with time travel logic. Quite a different sort of place, causally. And I've built the machine. I've distributed the blue prints far and wide, just recently, once I was sure it was for real. There's only one thing that could stop it. And it obviously has."

"I don't follow," I said.

"Any civilization that would have developed far enough to have time travel will always have had time travel. And we obviously don't, so we won't. We won't develop that far. This civilization is going to come to an end. It's going to collapse, perish, be destroyed before time travel starts. Tomorrow!"

"Who do you think is going to lob the first nuke," he continued. "The Chinese or the Caliphate?

"Oh my God," I said. "You can't believe that."

"Oh, you'll see," he said, rising and stumbling towards the door.

So here I am typing at my key-board in the middle of the night. It's daylight over there where the Caliphate and the Chinese are squabbling over India. And, oh my God, now I think I can hear the sirens starting to scream…

UNETHICAL FUNDS

Dave is a Financial Adviser. He is young and he is working in a large firm. He is also the victim of a motor vehicle accident. I've been treating him. He is almost better. Of course the insurance company is dicking us about... a bit. Before they cover his accident they are consuming his "extended benefits", so that once he has recovered they will have already whisked away his extended benefits saving themselves, collectively, a few hundred dollars. I think that little insurance company conspiracy might have been what set us off to invent the Unethical Fund. Or maybe we were talking about ethical stocks, while I was working on his neck, and one of us, or both of us, came up with the idea of a mutual fund based explicitly on "unethical stocks". I got quite excited. It would sell like hot cakes. Everyone assumes that unethical companies are profitable. We could make a million. "Dave's Devil's Own Unethical Fund". People would buy them as a novelty. You could put in one share of Enron. "Can you still buy Enron?" I asked.

"Oh yes. I believe it's selling at 39 cents this morning. And Anderson, of course," said Dave.

"Who are the big weapon's manufacturers?" I asked. "Besides Dow Chemicals."

"Not Dow. It's Lockheed and Boeing."

"How about General Motors?"

"General Electric. I don't know about General Motors," said Dave, "but certainly we can stick in Harley Davidson." Harley has been one of our favorite topics. It's America's new mother's milk and apple pie. There is a two-year waiting list to buy a bike.

"Why Harley?" I asked.

"Cause the Hell's Angels ride them. Think Harley, think Angels. And there's Exxon, B.P., Shell and their pollution. And the banks."

"And the insurance companies," I said.

"Oh, yes. The insurance companies for sure."

161

We added to our list with abandon. "There's McDonald's, for the trees and the heart disease."

"There's Talisman. A great Canadian firm." Just that week it had come public that Talisman had asked the Sudanese military to clear the villages out of the oil fields.

"And what about Volkswagen?" Dave asked.

"Actually," I said, "Volkswagen don't make any weapons on principle."

"Ah, but there was the Second World War slave labour."

"Well we could certainly throw in Krupt. I think they are big in pharmaceuticals nowadays, probably under some new name. We'll have to research the Second World War slave labour practices."

"What about pharmaceutical in general?" asked Dave.

"Well, I would think they are pretty unethical. That's a long story," I said. "I'll save it for another day, but Monsanto, and the other genetic engineering concerns, are a sure bet." Then I stopped and thought. "You know, maybe we could just pretend to buy unethical stocks and really by ethical stock. Tell everyone we were buying unethical, but cheat on them buy really buying ethical stocks. That would be unethical."

"And illegal," said Dave.

My enthusiasm for the project continued through to the end of our session, and through booking the next appointment, and seeing Dave to the door. I was sure Dave's Devil's Own Unethical Fund would be hot, would be viable. It could be a really big fad. Make us rich. But I sensed that, for Dave, this was not a serious proposition. He was just having fun. As he started down the stairs, I queried him. "You're not going to do this, are you? You know it would work. Everyone would buy some. Gifts for their friends. Just for a joke. We'd make a killing."

Dave looked back. "I don't really have time," he said. I'm too busy making money for my clients. And besides," he added, but then he left me hanging.

"And besides?" I asked.

"And beside… it would be unethical."

KUSALO'S OLD LADY

Ajahn Kusalo is a Buddhist monk in the "Thai Forrest" Theravadan tradition, and what a joy I found it to be in his company, to listen to him. A quiet laughter punctuates his speech and thoughts. He told a story I thought worth repeating...

Kusalo is from the antipodes, and his aged mother is in a Senior's Home in Australia. A while ago, during the general election, a candidate came to the Home soliciting the elderly resident's votes. He was talking to Kusalo's mum and another old lady and he perceived that old lady didn't seem to understand what he was doing there. "Do you know who I am?" he asked.

She reached out and touched his arm in reassurance. "No, Dear," she said, "but if you ask at the reception, they may be able to help you."

CODA: and I did repeat this story. Told it to many people, and on several occasions was told by some that they had heard the story before, variations on it. My God. The Buddhist say only speak that which passes the three gates: is it true, is it kind, is it useful.

I approached Ajahn Viadhamma about Kusalo's apparent untruth (that this happened to his mother).

"Oh, that Kusalo," said Ajahn V.

wikisays: *Nirvana / Nibbana* literally means
"blown out" like a candle

ni   out, without, away from
va   blow, as a wind; or waft as an odor
na   not, never, nor

van desire, love, win, possess, conquer,
       grasp, clench
van tree, thicket, quantity, wood
and *va* can mean weave

gatê gatê   gone gone

Nirvana Nibbana
wikisays: *Nirvana / Nibbana* means blown away
like a candle's flame

ni   out, without, away from
va   blow, as a wind; waft odor
na   not, never, nor

van desire, love, grasp,
van tree, thicket, quantity, wood
and *va* can mean weave

gatê gatê   *paragatê*   *parasamgatê*   *bodhi swaha*

Nirvana Nibbana
wikisays: it's literally "blown out"
like a candle

ni   out, without, away
va   blow, as a wind
na   not, never, nor

van desire, love, win, gain, procure, conquer, possess,
       grasp, clench
van tree, thicket, quantity, wood
va   weave

gatê gatê   gone

Made in the USA
Charleston, SC
11 July 2015